CRANNÓG 35   spring 2014

Editorial Board:

Sandra Bunting
Ger Burke
Jarlath Fahy
Tony O'Dwyer

ISSN 1649-4865
ISBN 978-1-907017-31-5

Cover image, 'La fuite', by Antoine Josse
Cover design by Sandra Bunting
Published by Wordsonthestreet for Crannóg Media
Printed in the UK

All writing copyrighted to rightful owners in accordance with The Berne Convention

Crannóg acknowledges the assistance of:

Galway City Council   Galway Language Centre   The Galway Study Centre

CONTENTS

FICTION

Home
   Siobhán Murtagh 8
Leisuredome
   Seán Kenny 13
Albert and Adelaide
   Joe Davies 18
The Vault of Heaven
   Mary Rose McCarthy 22
Lost
   Rebecca Stiffe 27
Last Order
   Martin Keaveney 30
Drenched
   Trisha McKinney 35
Worship
   Ruth Quinlan 40
The Holiday Photograph
   Padhraic Harris 43
Lovely Boy
   Madeline Parsons 46

POETRY

Grushie
   Breda Wall Ryan 52
That House
   Giles Newington 54
Cockle Picking
   Amanda Bell 55
Love Without Memory
   Maurice Devitt 56
The Night of Saint Lucy's Day
   D.S. Martin 57

Fuamnach Makes A Moth Of Etain
Ann Egan 58
Louise Latour
Patrick Maddock 60
Tulca
Aideen Henry 62
An Ghaoth Aduaidh
Fiona Nic Dhonnacha 63
Goodbye and Hello
Adam White 64
Necromancer
Amy Blythe 65
By the Landing's Light
C.P. Stewart 66
To Youth
Brian Kirk 67
On Reading the Glossary on the Lichens of Ireland Website
Sinéad Cotter 68
Recompense
Jean Tuomey 69
Winter Geese
Olivia Kenny McCarthy 70
In Sleep
Maria Bennett 71
Ringsend Water Music, 1983
Éamon Mag Uidhir 72
Treacle
Fiona Smith 73
Seasalt and Woodsmoke
Rachel Brownlow 74
Cartography
Luke Morgan 76
Bone
Timothy McLafferty 77
Rhapsody in Black
Mark Hart 78
Scribbles
Michael Farry 80
Tulips
Janet Shepperson 82

Necromancer
    Christopher Meehan 83
Kill Your Darlings
    Betsy Burke 84
The Canals on Mars
    Eamonn Lynskey 85
Look Up
    Shannon Quinn 86
Square Pegs
    Mark O'Flynn 87
Postcard from Tasmania
    Mark Mullee 88

Biographical Details 90

The Galway Study Centre

Since 1983, the Galway Study Centre has been dedicating itself to giving an excellent education service to post-primary school students in Galway.

info@galwaystudycentre.ie
Tel: 091-564254

www.galwaystudycentre.ie

BRIDGE MILLS
GALWAY LANGUAGE CENTRE
Established 1987

Small family run language school
ACELS and MEI RELSA approved
Courses in English, Italian, Polish, Portuguese, Spanish, German and Japanese
Teacher training including CELT TEFL

Telephone: +353 (0) 91 566 468 Fax: +353 (0) 91 564 122
Email: info@galwaylanguage.com

SUBMISSIONS

Crannóg is published three times a year in spring, summer and autumn.

Submission Times: Month of November for spring issue. Month of March for summer issue. Month of July for autumn issue.

We will not read *submissions sent outside these times*.

POETRY: Send no more than three poems. Each poem should be under 50 lines.

PROSE: Send one story. Stories should be under 2,000 words.

We do not accept postal submissions.

When emailing your submission we require three things:

1. The text of your submission included both in body of email and as a Word attachment (this is to ensure correct layout. We may, however, change your layout to suit our publication).
2. A brief bio in the third person. Include this both in body and in attachment.
3. A postal address for contributor's copy in the event of publication.

To learn more about Crannóg Magazine, or purchase copies of the current issue, log on to our website:

www.crannogmagazine.com

FICTION

HOME   SIOBHÁN MURTAGH

Late one August evening I packed my holdall and stood in the hallway of my friend's flat. He and his girlfriend had been arguing for hours behind their bedroom door, with my name the bullet in their crossfire. By the time their voices had softened, I was waiting at the door. Rob emerged, biting his lip and looking at the floor.

'It's alright,' I said, 'I understand.'

He nodded.

'But where will you go?'

'Rob. Don't worry about me,' I laughed. 'It's not as if I'm not going to end up on the streets.'

Outside the air was muggy, the grey sky squatting low over the buildings. I headed towards the city centre, pushing against the flow of workers going home. And where *would* I go? It was two days until my jobseeker's was due, and even then it wouldn't cover a B & B. I couldn't ask any other friends to put me up after the hassle with Rob, and my parents were out of the question. I kept taking money out of my pocket and looking at it, hoping by some miracle there would be more.

And then the rain started, fat icy drops, shockingly cold against my skin. I passed a steamy café, still open for late-night shoppers, and went in. I ordered tea and a glass of water and drank them slowly, the tea stewed and cold by the time I had finished. The place was warm and sticky and already I regretted not having showered and shaved in Rob's. On TV a man was talking about how he'd been made redundant, how he'd given his best for over thirty years. I turned away and leant my head against the misted window. Rivers of condensation ran down the pane: some rapid, some slow until they gathered weight and then hurtled towards the finish like a sprinter. With my finger I traced the letter 'A' among their crooked paths.

When the café closed I wandered on to the street. Damp footpaths glowed beneath the shop windows. I walked until my legs grew heavy. Darkness fell in on the city. I passed an alleyway and entered it. It was empty but smelled of vomit. It seemed at that moment that there was nowhere better for me to be, so I threw my bag on the ground and sat down. The wall was rough against my back. My stomach felt sick with tiredness but my brain was wired. An ambulance sped by, its siren tearing through the quiet. Then the sound of some drunks shouting and laughing. One of them stepped in to the alley. I pressed myself into the darkness and stayed still. He shuffled and breathed noisily. I heard the zip of his fly. The sharp tang of urine reached my nostrils. Above me I could see a patch of pale, starless sky. I thought of how dark that same sky would be right now over my parents' farm.

Since then I have been sleeping against the goods entrance of a shop. It's down a laneway so no one I know will see me. When I doze my dreams are hazy with crowded streets and faceless people, pointing at me. There is another dream I have – a bedroom, cool and smelling of polish and laundered sheets. Strangely, it is not the bedroom of my married home, but my old bedroom in my parents' house; even though it is years since I lived there.

One night the sound of footsteps roused me. I pulled back my jacket to see a young guy standing over me, his red eyes blinking in slow motion, his face unshaven. He fiddled in his coat pocket. I sat up, my heart thumping. Then his lips moved, as if he was rehearsing how to speak.

'Ssss....Sss....Story, Bud,' he said.

'Story,' I said.

'Any smokes?'

I shook my head.

His lip curled up, as if he had expected more of me.

'Fuck that,' he said and he huddled into the opposite corner and went to sleep.

It felt strange when I woke to find him staring at me, pulling on a cigarette.

'I thought you had no smokes,' I said.

'I'd be a sorry bastard not to ask,' he laughed.

Roy was his name. He showed me a gap between two buildings where I could hide my bag, a cheap place to eat near Connolly, and where to score any sort of drug that might take my fancy.

At night the cold burrows its way in to your bones like a virus. The sun is getting lower over the Liffey and in the Green there is a dryness to the leaves. Already there are queues outside the hostels. One night I went and stood outside one, the smell of beefy soup drifting out. Through the window I saw a wizened man cradling a mug in his dusty hands. I took a step forward, and then stopped. It seemed too unbelievable that I would belong in such a place, and so I left.

It doesn't take long for the filth of the city to stick to you. There is a secret layer of grime that you never knew existed. It embeds itself in your skin until one day you look in a mirror and see that you are altered. Roy says that I should try to find a squat. I should try to find a job, that's what I should do. In my last place they announced the job cuts and the following day they called us in one by one, to go through what they called the Matrix, a test to see how we all performed in comparison to each other. All day long we eyed each other in a newly suspicious way, like fighting cocks. I was secretly confident: I was never late, never sick, did what was asked of me, always. At five o'clock they sent for me.

'I'm very sorry,' said a potbellied man whose neck spilled out over his shirt collar.

In our section the two people with the lowest scores had to go. I was one of them. Poor team-building attitude, they said. Low marks for interpersonal skills. It was like something broke inside me, like eggs had smashed and their contents had pooled in my stomach. Since then it's been like trying to gather this slime up with my hands, to render myself whole again. And I'm tired, so very tired.

Some nights, Roy brings other guys down the lane. The talk is of who was moved on, who was picked up, who got lucky. Often they use words that I don't even understand. One night someone offered me a 'disco biscuit'.

'Yeah, thanks,' I said. 'I'm starving.'

Their laughter stirred up the dank air and bounced off the walls until one of them shouted, 'Stop! I'm going to wet myself.'

Roy grinned at me and shook his head. 'You're some Dalkeyite,' he said.

And still, despite this strange new language, I get the message. Someday they're going to get off the drugs, the booze, the game: get the right doctor, get the right meds, get the right dose, find the right scheme, find a good place, a job, a partner – find a life. I had a life, had all those things; and yet they vanished through my fingers, fragile as the morning cobwebs on the park gates.

Roy asks, 'Here, have ye no family to give you a leg up?'

But no way am I turning to my parents. Not after everything they did for me when Vicky told me she was pregnant, at just twenty-one. Not after they gave us the deposit for the house and a small wedding and a bit of money in the post office for Aoife when she was born. I had to borrow from them when the judge ruled in favour of Vicky keeping the house – just to get a place of my own. After that, I swore that no way would I ask them again, and I haven't. I won't speak to anyone from my old life, not until I'm sorted.

Last week I saw my cousin Billy. He was walking up Parnell Street chatting to a friend, his suit crumpled and eyes heavy with the satisfied weariness of a day's work. I was hunkered down outside a shop, bothering nobody, when a security man came out and nudged me with the toe of his boot.

'Get outta here,' he said loudly.

I saw Billy glance back, and then stop and turn around. I gathered myself and ran in the opposite direction, sensing him staring after me as I weaved through the crowd.

I have a photo of Aoife that I always carry in my pocket. If I lost that photo I don't know what I would do. Most of my jobseeker's goes straight to her and I would give more if I could; only you can't send coins in the post. When I lived in the flat she came on Fridays and we would play twister and drink cream soda and eat pot noodles.

Last Christmas, before my redundancy money ran out, I took her to the pantomime. In the sweet-smelling darkness we threw back our heads and laughed and shouted, 'She's behind you!' at the top of our voices. I watched her, the coloured lights bouncing off her skin, her small teeth gleaming in the dimness. When I hid my face behind my hands in mock terror she patted me on the arm and said, 'Don't worry, Daddy, I'll mind you.'

Later, while she picked at nuggets and chips, I winked at her, just for the pleasure of seeing her dimples when she smiled back. We were quiet together, a happy tiredness between us. She slid off her chair and climbed up on my lap. I held her, aware of the slightness of her bones beneath my hands. Then she looked up.

'You're nice, Daddy,' she said, a small crease appearing between her eyebrows.

Her words seemed to gouge out a hollow in my chest. I wanted to scream, 'I'm *not*. I messed up. I messed *everything* up.' But instead I pulled her closer and buried my face into her strawberry-scented hair.

The other day, walking down Grafton Street, I caught that scent wafting from a shop that sells soaps. I stopped dead on the footpath. People had to walk around me to pass.

'Weirdo,' someone muttered as they brushed by.

During the evening rush hour I sit in the shelter of steps on Capel Street. I close my eyes and feel the shadows of the walkers changing the light behind my eyelids. After a while one shadow darkens the space. The light doesn't follow. The shadow has stopped.

'Joseph,' I hear.

I open my eyes and she is in front of me, my father standing behind her. She stoops and runs her fingertips along my bearded cheek. I close my eyes and keep them closed.

'Joseph,' she says again.

Hot tears seep out between my eyelids. I feel her warm hand against my face, her thumb wiping them away. I shake my head.

'I can't,' I say. 'No way.'

She nods slowly. 'Alright then,' she says. 'We'll just stay here, with you.' And she catches up her skirt and eases herself onto the urine-stained ground. My father sits on a step and rubs his chin in that old patient way. Her hand is soft on top of mine. After a time, it is too hard not to lean my weight against her, and so I do.

LEISUREDOME

SEÁN KENNY

He wants you to know that he's not a violent man. Okay? People have actually referred to him as a gentle giant. A *gentle* giant, right? Not 'a homicidal giant' or 'a giant with a restraining order out against him'. Gentle. Because he is. Virtually all of the time. We're talking, probably 99.999 per cent of his existence here, yeah? It was *her*, pushing all his buttons like that.

And now he gets to see his little boy when? Never, that's when.

Yeah, well. He loves that kid. *Josh*, he has tattooed on the inside of his left wrist. Three months now since the case. He posted Josh a mobile with a little note explaining how to work the phone and saying he'd call him. Two days later he phoned and it wasn't the kid who answered. No. Guess who? Sandra, letting fly with language that'd make a sailor blush. You would not believe the abuse. He tried saying he just wanted to talk to his son but she said he had no right to call Josh his son. That, and a lot of words beginning with f and b. One beginning with c and all. He hung up. It was like she lit this fuse in him. But he did his breathing exercises like he learnt in the sessions and, no, for your information, your *honour*, he didn't punch anything this time.

So he's got a plan. He thought about trying the school, maybe collecting Josh a little early before the grandparents got there. But the school would know. There were no flies on Sandra. She'd have given them all the gory details, spiced up with all sorts of slanderous lies no doubt, the bitch.

But he has his means. Gerry, a mate of his, has a kid on Josh's football team so he asked when and where their next match was. Gerry looked at him, brow creased, all worried, like.

'Is it just to watch the match?'

He thought about how to answer this.

'Yeah, just to watch. I'll keep at a distance. Look, I just want to see him.'

'Are you sure that's a good idea? I mean, with everything...'

'Look, imagine it was your kid. How would you feel? I haven't seen him in months.' He got a little teary here, cos it burns at him. Like acid in his gut. He turned his head away.

'All right. I'm trusting you here. Don't make me regret this.'

So Gerry texted him. But it was disappointing, how he had to pull the info out of him like an old tooth. He'd be having words with Gerry in the not-too-distant future. Words like *loyalty* and *friendship*. Gerry's wife, she was mates with Sandra. She was even poisoning his friends against him now.

So he's driving to the match, flooring it down the dual carriageway and Oasis shaking the speakers. He's singing, belting it out, cos it's a top tune and he's feeling good. *Don't look back in anger, I heard you say.*

Sandra never hangs around. She drops Josh off and picks him up. She'll be off breathing fire from her nostrils over litters of new-born puppies or something.

The team manager; he's taking a bit of a risk there. Might know. But it's worth taking the chance. It's important not to think too much about it, cos it messes with his head and he gets all on edge. He *ruminates*, that's what your one says in the sessions.

He steals an odd look at the small mountain of bars, the Carrauntoohil of chocolate on the passenger seat, and smiles. Twix, Mars, Kit-Kat, Snickers, Aero, Mint Aero, Galaxy, Galaxy Caramel, not forgetting the Cadbury's contingent of Turkish Delight and Dairy Milk. He probably shouldn't give him that much, but fuck it, he'd spoil the lad for a day.

He pulls up at the pitches and looks out across the grass for a moment – he likes the colour green; it's calm – before there's a click and clunk of car door and he's striding out.

Keeps his distance, he does, during the game. Not easy to keep a low profile when you're six foot four. Half-time whistle cuts the air and he's walking over to Josh. Kid's eyes are out on stalks. Well, of course he's surprised. Hasn't seen his dad in ages, poor lad.

'Hey, Josh! How's it going, buddy?'

Kid's speechless.

'Look, I know those people wanted to stop me seeing you, but they don't know me, those people. Who knows me better, them or you?'

Thinks about this, Josh does.

'Me.'

'See?'

The manager, little prick of a busybody, he's steaming over, then. 'Hello, can I help you there? Josh, are you okay?'

'No, sorry. I didn't have a chance to introduce myself. I'm Josh's dad. I'm afraid there's a family emergency. Thanks a million for looking after him and everything. You have a sub, don't you? Thanks, talk to you later.'

He grabs Josh's bag. Then they're in the car. He makes sure Josh has his seatbelt on, cos he's being responsible, your *honour*. Spins around, he does, big grin plastered across his musher, and tosses Josh one of the bars. It catches him in the eye, though. His little hand flips up to it, rubbing like he's hurt. Doesn't cry, though, doesn't make a sound.

'Aw, Josh. No, Josh, look, that was an accident. I'm sorry, son.' Nods, he does, after a spell. He's a good lad.

'Go on, the bar's for you.'

'I don't like chocolate.'

Kids. It's all phases, isn't it?

'Ah, you'll have one. A Kit-Kat, even. There's hardly any chocolate in that.'

He holds the bar out. Josh takes the bar. It's all phases.

They're on their way to that big place near the shopping centre. Leisuredome, it's called. Josh'll love it. Bowling, pool, air hockey, slot machines, video games. He throws an eye at the rear view. Shivering, Josh is.

'Are you cold, Josh? It's cos you were running around and now you've stopped. Here, put this over you,' and he's grabbing a rain jacket when they're stopped at lights. He doesn't want him getting sick.

Josh is still shivering after he's put the jacket on, though. Which is weird. Might be coming down with something. Still, they swing into the Leisuredome car park. It'll be warm inside, warm and bright. There's a cheerful chirp and ping of video games and the clack of snooker balls and the lovely low rumble of bowling balls down the alley. They get their bowling shoes. Sizes 12 and 4. Josh's shoes are so small next to his that he almost tears up but he holds it together. Deep breaths, like your one showed him.

Starts off okay, it does. He scores an eight, then a half-strike. But Josh, he's guttering every ball. So he decides to help him, take his arm and guide him through the next shot. He's just approaching him, though, when Josh flinches, *cowers* even, is that the word? And this bloke in the next alley, he's staring over at them, his brow all creased, sticking his beak right in it, he is.

The feeling bubbles up through him just like that. He turns around to your man. 'Are you all right there? I'm just having a game of bowling with my son, yeah? So mind your own *fucking business, yeah?*' The last three words leave him like they're rocket-fuelled. Powered by red-hot rage. Josh is crying, then. He goes to put an arm round Josh and he does the flinching thing again.

He wants to go back in time. Rewind life. But he can't. All he has is today, his chocolate and his bowling. Josh stops crying, but he keeps guttering the ball. He has a face on him like he's licked shite off a shoe heel.

Josh is going to have fun. He's breaking the law here, so Josh can have fun. Josh *has to* have fun. So he asks him what he wants to do next. A driving game? Pool? Air hockey?

Maybe Josh is tired but all he does is shrugs. So he finds this game where you throw a basketball at a hoop. Slides some coins into the slot, he does.

'Throw it,' he says and he puts the ball in Josh's hands. He just wants him to have fun. Josh throws the ball. He misses. The ball rolls back.

'Another one,' he says and Josh picks it up himself this time.

'And again.' He doesn't have to say anything after that. Kid keeps throwing the ball and he keeps feeding coins into the slot. He's a good lad.

He just wants his little boy to have fun. 'Are you tired?' he asks and Josh shakes his head. He is, though, he's tired. Kids never want to admit they're tired. That bitch of a mother of his, not making sure he's getting enough sleep.

Then they play air hockey. Of course, he's going to let Josh win. But it's well weird cos it's like Josh is trying not to win either. He scores accidentally a few times and ends up winning.

It's not exactly how he planned the day.

When they get back to the car a lot of the chocolate has melted. He turns his phone on and it's just like he expected. Twenty-eight missed calls from Sandra. Typical over-reaction. She'd have a SWAT team on him, she would, if she had her way. And for what? For taking his boy to the Leisuredome.

And how do you plead?

I plead guilty to the crime of taking my boy out to have some fun. So shoot me.

He pulls up on Sandra's road, a safe distance from the gaff. He's just turning round to say goodbye to Josh but all he catches is a flash of tracksuit. Josh is gone, he's left the chocolate behind and it's like a knife in his heart. He pulls away from the kerb fairly sharpish.

The guards will be round to him. He's going to say he doesn't accept the court's decision. That he's a changed man. There won't be any shouting or kicking of wing mirrors. Not this time. He's going to ask them, right, this is his killer line, he's going to ask them –

Well, was I violent? Did Josh say I was violent? Well, did he?

ALBERT AND ADELAIDE   JOE DAVIES

They had made a home together and tried hard to keep it that way. It was clean. The rent was paid regularly, as regularly as could be expected under the circumstances. The walls were not cluttered but the two of them had prided themselves on the few pieces of art they'd bought since being together, work by local artists working en plein air. Recently, though, there'd come to be empty spaces, paintings sold to help cover the shortfalls they'd been encountering.

Their names were Albert and Adelaide and they were not married but long-time partners and everyone who knew them said their names together in one breath as if that was how you spoke of them, as one entity. Albert and Adelaide at the movies together. Albert and Adelaide on a canoe trip. Albert and Adelaide know how to throw a dinner party. She had a great smile, he a receding hairline that made him look distinguished. They looked good, but slowly, slowly, they were becoming impoverished. Looking in on their lives from the outside no one might ever have guessed. And the few who saw the edges beginning to fray couldn't have suspected why.

So here, come inside. And have a look.

It is a quarter to five in the morning and the lights are all out. The bedroom is dark. The sheets are soft and the pillow feels good just the way it is, folded under at the edge. Albert is content. This is one of the things he cherishes most, the luxury of sleep. He rolls over and curls up towards Adelaide and he reaches and reaches and his hand runs out across the smooth sheet until he feels the edge of the bed and his eyes open.

She's not there.

'Damn,' he mumbles half asleep into his pillow. 'Not again.'

He sits upright, swings his legs from under the blankets, and reaches for the telephone. He calls for a cab. By the time it arrives he is dressed and has had a piece of toast with raspberry jam spread thinly across it. Everything is coming to be spread thinly these days, he thinks. Some because they are trying, others because it can't be helped.

'Good morning,' says the cab driver as Albert slips into the back. The cabbie smells of mouthwash or some other medicinal thing and for some reason Albert finds this faintly troubling.

'Good morning,' says Albert, business-like.

'And where are we going?' asks the driver.

Albert tells him and they set out.

The streets are wet though it is no longer raining, and the sky is clear to the west. As they set off along the 115 Albert's gaze settles on the full moon, down near the horizon. It shines brightly, with an almost hypnotising intensity. No matter how many times he does this, it always feels strange to have set out in the dark. He is awake, and knows it, and it feels clichéd to even think it, but it's like being in a dream. The night gliding past, the spareness of the traffic, the headlights of the cab unearthing the road before it rolls underneath the wheels like some gigantic conveyer belt.

The cab takes the off-ramp to Highway 28 and turns south. Towards the east it is now possible to make out the sky beginning to brighten, the outline of the retreating clouds faint but distinct.

They talk, Albert and the cabbie. He is okay but a little depressing, has a daughter he has not seen since she was eleven.

'She was the cutest thing,' he says. 'Must be twenty-eight now.'

'That's very sad,' says Albert. 'I'm sorry.'

'My wife soured her against me. I try to get in touch but never get anywhere. She's got it in her head that I'm some kind of an ogre. And that's that.'

What Albert thinks he will not say, since what he thinks is that this, like the feeling of being in a dream, is also a commonplace, so he says nothing.

'Hold 'em close while you can,' recites the cabbie. 'Cause they might not always be there.'

Before they turn into the drive leading up to the racetrack, Albert takes a last glance at the brightening sky to the east. It is beautiful. In a short while, a matter of minutes, it ought to make a good subject for a painting. If all goes smoothly, and he has no reason to doubt it will, he will see it on his way back out of the building.

Stepping out of the cab at the brightly lit doors of the racetrack, Albert says to the cabbie that if he's still there in about ten minutes there'll be a return trip into town. 'And if not,' he says, 'I hope you hear from your daughter. Someday.'

The cabbie nods. Albert closes the door and watches as the taxi pulls forward a little and stops.

She stands at one of the slot machines, twigs in her hair, her bare, muddied feet looking slim and vulnerable beneath the hem of her nightdress. She stands on tip-toe, her one arm steadying her, the other repetitively pulling the arm of the shiny machine.

And of course, she is asleep.

How many times has Adelaide done this? Albert has never kept track. A few dozen perhaps.

A sign on the far wall, which reads 'No Sleep Walkers', is apparently an empty gesture, as it is not enforced and those who find themselves in that soporific state are unlikely to make sense of such a sign even if they did read it.

Albert approaches her quietly, and very slowly, very gently, begins to talk to her, suggesting what they should do next, how she should come with him, how there's a warm bed in a loving home waiting for her, how she should do what he is asking because it is best. And before long his words have the desired effect on her, and she turns and comes with him. They walk past the rows of machines and past other people standing there, some of them also with muddy feet and twigs in their hair, staring at what's before them with unseeing eyes.

The brightening horizon, as Albert suspected, is stunning, and the cab has waited after all.

Albert and Adelaide get into the back. Albert and Adelaide lean against one another. Albert continues to talk in comforting tones, and Adelaide, asleep, is soothed.

He talks quietly. He says, 'And these are the things we do together. We like to go to the market. And we like to buy fresh bread. We like to eat it by the river and tear off pieces for one another. And when we first met we went to see a parade on George Street, the Canada Day parade. And your favourite movie is my favourite movie. And I will stay with you no matter what.'

And when they arrive home and Albert leans in to pay the cab driver, the cabbie, who has been listening all the way, wipes his eyes and says he will not accept any money and drives away. And all Albert can think is that every little bit helps these days.

In the morning Albert and Adelaide sit across from each other eating breakfast and reading the paper, and Adelaide produces a twig from behind her ear which Albert somehow missed, and she says, 'Look at this, Albert. Where on earth do you think this came from?' And she is genuinely surprised. For she does not know. He has never said.

Albert, his paper lowered, smiles at her and says, 'Sumach?'

Behind her, on the wall, is the painting he will have to sell next.

'What do you think?' she says, the hint of a sparkle in her tired eyes. 'Am I leading a double life?'

THE VAULT OF HEAVEN　　　MARY ROSE MCCARTHY

The rope groans and creaks in Malachy's calloused hands. It is hardened and sodden from years of salt water labour. Years of hauling fish ashore by net, years of standing waist-deep in freezing water. And for what, wonders Malachy? Can a man's life be measured in a fish catch?

The tendons on his neck and arms bulge and stand to attention, as the weight settles and solidifies, fish, flapping frantically, men shouting manically, 'heave, heave, heave ashore boys. Nearly there now boys.'

Malachy digs his heels in the dun-coloured sand, tries to get a purchase in the softness, moves back an inch or two and hauls the booty nearer to shore. His opposite anchor on his right is doing the very same. Imperceptibly moving back, dragging the rope, dotted at intervals with other men all straining, sensing rather than seeing, the end in sight.

Out in the deep, where the net makes the perfect curve of a semi-circle, Murph treads water, guiding and holding the depth, ensuring that not one precious fish manages to swim away. Murph calls the instructions, moves along the circumference of the net, hand over hand.

Murph can't swim – none of the fishermen ever learn. There is an old tradition here that the ability to swim will only prolong a slow agonising death, if the sea has it in mind to claim a man. And every so often the sea does demand its ransom. So the men believe it is better to relinquish their grip on life should their time come, better to succumb to the lap and suck, the pull and tug, of a water that never rests.

Malachy senses less resistance in the rope; it is slowly relenting and acquiescing to the struggle of the men. His feet move backwards step by quickening step; Murph is looming from the depths. The first of the fish gasps against the sand, desperately trying to stay in the inch of tide. In unison the men's final heave brings the net full clear of the water. They sink on the sand sentinels around their final, panting prize. Exhausted, they look one to the other and smile, no energy for words. It has been a good day. The vastness of the vault of heaven, streaked with white clouds, catches Malachy's attention.

Malachy walks home alone. The other men have stayed behind to sort and gut and grade and box the fish. More cold, hard work, that Malachy can't bring himself to do. He knows this will mean less divvied out to him but he can't allow himself to think of that now.

It's that vast sky Malachy wants to capture. He was born to paint – watercolours, oils, anything. But there is no living to be had from painting, the mouths of offspring always demanding, food or clothes, or just plain demanding.

'Who ever dreams of growing up to be a fisherman?' Malachy has asked his wife on more than one winter's evening, when they are sequestered by the fire, nature trapping them indoors.

Her only answer – a sigh from the depths saying it all and more. Saying we've been over this before, what's the use of what ifs? It is as it is, and we've responsibilities now, making do and stretching. There is never enough. Enough food or money but most of all, for Malachy, there is never enough light or time.

And this evening, with the sky so blue and the sea so calm, Malachy is determined to carve out time. Sneaking into the house, he checks if any of them are back yet from school or town; he never keeps track of where they spend their days. The stairs creak as usual on the third step, an echo of the groaning rope of earlier. Creaks and groans, musical regrets peppering his life.

Shrugging himself from the still moist salt-stiff clothes, he pulls dry ones from the wardrobe and leaves the bedroom in a mess of his divested fisherman self. He grabs his paints and paper, donning his artist persona. Putting on his true self. Within minutes he is back on the same shore, the same sand and sea; but a mile further downstream from the fish and the screaming gulls and the work. The dreaded, hateful work.

Pulling pipe and tobacco from his pocket he fills the bowl, tamping the shreds of tobacco down, taking his time, anticipating the satisfaction of the first draw. The smell mingles with the salt-air tang, the first lungful burns and then settles as if flowing into the very marrow of his bones.

At the height of hauling the fish earlier he spied the other boat. Those well-heeled, well-dressed people, with nothing better to do than putter about on the river all day long. One of the women on-board wore something red, the colour vivid in his mind's eye. She was standing, lone and alone, in the stern as the men pottered on the pebbly shore. Perhaps he can depict it, paint them as they are, blissfully oblivious to the motley crew of men hauling and heaving nets ashore.

His hands, coarsened and stiffened, are clumsy as he opens up the sketch pad. The wind has come up now, stinging his cheeks and ruffling the pages. It is a nice sound; paper rustling in the wind. But it is a moisture-laden breeze which also ruffles the sea, whipping horses' heads into view. His pencil digs into the mist-softened paper. The lines won't flow; the whole he saw in his mind's eye now smudged and blurred.

The well-to-do leisure party have weighed anchor. He can hear the rhythmic tutter of the engine. They've read the signs in the mackerel sky, know that heavier winds and rains are on the way. Malachy watches in despair and disgust, as the boat moves up-stream towards the city and comfort, leaving, momentarily, a white stream in its wake. His day is now wasted, the vault of heaven quickly closed over, with the lowering, grey clouds of another soft, Irish day. Too late to join his fishermen colleagues and attempt to claim a larger share of the day's labours.

Orange flames lick the pub's turf fire into life. Meagre warmth is beginning to seep out into the bar where Malachy perches on a stool at the counter, contemplating his third pint. The swirl of black as it spirals and settles into the creamy top echoes the swirl and bubbling of the ocean as it eventually gave up its bounty this afternoon. In a battered leather satchel at his feet are the papers and paints, the trinkets and trappings of another unlived life. Abandoning his art, due to the adverse weather, he settles for the pub, the comfort and succour of alcohol to dull the edges. The other men at the counter ignore Malachy, his aura of despair warding off company, enclosing him in his own semi-circle of misery.

He orders a whiskey chaser, the amber glow mirroring the warm tones of the fire. The peat-filtered drink seeps and soaks into his pores, thawing the salt-stiffened joints, dulling the pain in his soul.

There is a rumour that a French craft will be in town next week. In the warm glow of whiskey Malachy sees what life might be like in Paris for an artist. The freedom and space and weather for painting; art and creativity wafting in off the Seine. His humble needs would be so easily met in France – some bread and cheese, a palette and paints. Perhaps the occasional bottle of red wine. Lost in contemplation, Malachy is not aware of the door opening, or the fog-wet draught swirling in around the drinkers' ankles.

'So this is where you are. As usual. Drinking it all away before you even get

paid. Losing the catch in the depths of the glass. Come on home. With you. Now.'
And his wife crooks her arm under his elbow and steers and pushes him through the throng of smirking onlookers. As he staggers into the night air, Paris and art, bread and cheese evaporate.

'I told you before, every time you go off spending money we don't have I'll come and get you. It doesn't bother me who sees, or what they think for that matter. Let them talk. We've children to feed. Something you conveniently forget. And by the way, I met Murph coming down the road. On his way to pay out your share. He gave it to me.'

Blinded with alcohol, misery and rage, Malachy follows his wife up the half-mile hill to home. He can see the indignation bristling from her shoulders as she walks. There is no money for him. There is nothing for him. His satchel of painting materials jags against his left leg with each uneven step, mocking his dreams, his needs for more. More than this, this life lived on the edge of seas and rivers, fishing for food, never catching dreams.

The sea, the family, his children, trap him. His wife colludes with his gaffer to pay the wages directly to her, so he can't squander them on porter and whiskey. Her words. Neither now can he invest them in getting away to France. Watercolour worlds, skies seeping into rain-filled clouds, barley fields framing gunmetal rivers, none of this is meant for him. It taunts and teases him, beguiles and beckons, but is always too distant to grasp.

Halfway up the hill he pauses, shuddering to catch his breath, his dreams and visions leaching from him in sobs as he bends over, putting his hands on his knees. Not caring, or not seeing, his wife marches on, virtuous in her newly won battle, proud that one of them is taking their responsibilities seriously. Malachy straightens up, staring at his wife's retreating figure. Despite the distance, he still senses her self-righteousness. With a massive heave and animal-like bellow he lobs the satchel over the furze-shrouded hill.

For a moment it hovers, caught on a bush. In the half-moonlight it looks grotesque, a battered, brown, bug-like creature about to devour the plant on which it settles. The wind sighs, rustling the branches, unsnagging the burden.

The up-draught catches his materials, his dreams and passions, and sends them sailing into the careless, continuous swell of the sea far below. Boating parties in colour, studios on the Parisian left bank, weigh it down sufficiently to fill up and sink. Malachy continues the trudge on home.

'You needn't think I kept you any dinner,' his wife says as soon as he's through the door. Later in bed she humps her body into a tight coil, making an S shape away from him, as sibilant as any hiss.

Towards first light she prods him awake. His tongue, furred and dry, is stuck to the roof of his mouth. In the morning dusk he sees he still wears yesterday's clothes.

'Get up,' his wife says. 'Murph said they want to make an early start today, there's a big school of trout out around the point. He thinks it will push in on the morning tide. Be sure to turn up, Murph said.'

Malachy stumbles from the bed, reclaims his dried-out, stiff-as-boards fishing clothes from where he discarded them on the floor in yesterday afternoon's urgency to capture the light. At the back door, he draws on the heavy boots which drag his footsteps, as he faces downhill to join the other men waiting on the sand which crunches under foot. Each crunch splinters Malachy's hangover as his boots splinter the salt-crusted shore. The men chafe their calloused hands, gruff hellos to each other from under cap-shaded eyes. Malachy waits with them for Murph to pay out the rope and assemble the crew before they wade, waist deep, into the jade-green water. Men are dotted at intervals along the rope like beads on a rosary. They cling to the damp, thick strands as if it is a lifeline.

LOST   REBECCA STIFFE

'Wait, Mum, where are you going?' asks Pam, dashing towards me from the kitchen, tea towel flailing behind her.

'I'm just going down to O'Hara's to get some sausages for tea. Do you want anything, love?' I ask, throwing on my headscarf and fetching the tattered yellow umbrella from beneath the rickety stairs. It was a beautiful day, but you never know with our kind of weather. The sun is splitting the rocks one minute, pouring cats and dogs the next.

I glance up at Pam. A worrying look envelopes her face and her brow is furrowed. Her hands are arched on her hips and I know exactly what she is thinking; she's so predictable.

'Maybe Jim should go with you, you know ... just for the walk. Jim!' She calls for her husband.

'Nonsense,' I dismiss, 'I may be old, but I'd like to think I'm not going senile just yet. I most certainly *do not* need a babysitter. Thank you very much, Jim dear, all the same.' And with that, I amble out the door without a second glance, ignoring their persistent pleas.

On the way to the butcher's, I decide to take a peaceful walk along the city basin to feed the ducks. It's always so peaceful out on the basin. I like to watch the furry grey cygnets dive down beneath the murky water and disappear, trying to decipher where they might resurface. They're so unpredictable, and I love it. The water is still and quiet. The only movement is of the gentle V-shaped ripples trailing behind the birds as they glide effortlessly over the surface. Closing my eyes, the only sounds to be heard are the creaking of boughs against the gentle autumn breeze, the larks chirping high up above as they soar across a cloudless sky and the soft but continuous rustling of the bushes, all intertwining to create an intricate and irrecoverable melody of nature. There's a certain tranquillity and serenity that comes with reflecting next to the basin that I can never quite explain well enough to anyone to do it justice.

As I walk out of the park, I notice it's beginning to get dark. The trees loom hauntingly over the scattered avenues and the gentle breeze has transformed into an eerie draught. The streets are empty and I don't recognise where I am. Nervously, I begin down the abandoned road. From the dim of the streetlights I can just about make out a dark silhouette staggering towards me. As the light falls on his face I can see him more clearly. He has a rugged beard and oversized clothing hanging from his body. His expression is grim but his glazed eyes can't focus on me – or anything else for that matter. Clutching my umbrella tight, I wait and anticipate what this man might do next. He stumbles and slouches onto the high fence bordering the park – now infested with unrecognisable shadows. As he mutters something to a hydrangea, I quicken my pace and sidestep him, aiming to put as much space between us as I can.

At the end of the street, I come to a crossroads. Completely unsure of which route to take, I analyse both and decide to veer left, primarily because it has more streetlights. I'm beyond frightened. The fear of the unknown is overwhelming in this alien place. When a car turns up the road towards me I feel like a deer caught in the headlights. I use my elbow to shield my light-sensitive eyes and continue walking, not sure where I plan to end up. My heart rate quickens as the car begins to slow down towards me. I continue walking past the car. I hear car doors opening and slamming shut and footsteps following me. I try to walk faster but my old hips are acting up again and they won't let me.

I can hear the footsteps gaining on me as they echo off the vacant boulevard. Just as my hips are about to give way, a large hand grabs my elbow and pulls me around.

'It's alright, Rose. Relax.'

'Who are you?' I scream into the man's face. How does he know my name? His voice is alarmingly calm.

'Just come with us, Rose, you'll be alright.'

'I'm not going anywhere with you! Let go!' I panic as I try to pull away from him but he won't let me go. There's a young, thin woman crying hysterically behind him. Who are these people? What are they trying to do to me?

'Call Doctor Walker, love, tell him we're on our way,' he says to the woman as she nods and dials a number on her phone. I frantically call for help to anyone who might be around, but it's no use. My cries echo off the emptiness that surrounds us.

'I promise you'll be fine. Just get in the car, please,' he asks again, but he gives me no choice as he pushes me firmly into the car and gets in on the other side. Heart pumping, I begin to pound on the windows and pull at the door handle but again, it's no use. I'm trapped. I push myself up against the door and sit as far away from the strange man as possible.

'I'm sorry, Rose. My name is Jim,' he says, his arm extended. Reluctantly I shake his hand. His voice is still calm and undisturbed. He points to the woman. 'This is my wife–'

'Pam, dear,' I exclaim. 'What on earth are you crying about?'

LAST ORDER   MARTIN KEAVENEY

There was one more call to make on the back road, a long and hilly trail through a remote townland in the south-east corner of the parish. The home of Walter Reilly, yet another of the village's numerous elderly bachelors. Reilly was unusual in that he did not own a bicycle and walked everywhere, particularly to the local pub, where he was to be found most nights. The boy pondered on the evening's sales as he cycled the final ascent.

Since he was nine, his father had annually entrusted him with the village door-to-door sales of the Christmas Club raffle, selling them at 50p each and three tickets for a pound. The most exciting part was the club's allowance of the seller to keep the extra 50p from each book individually sold. On this route – bachelors, widows, characters whose marital status was questionable – the single ticket purchase was popular. It meant the boy's inside pocket rattled with £4.50 of commission. He looked forward to visiting Sweeney's travelling shop on Friday where he would convert it into Macaroon bars, a bag of Chickatees and a small bottle of fizzy cola.

Reilly's house was hidden beneath a thick veneer of gorse and long, jungle-like grass. Years of failure to cut what had probably once been a proud front garden had resulted in wild plants, joining together and mutating higher than the first slate on the roof. The house, too, had suffered years of neglect; ivy crawled messily across one whole gable and now threatened the front window. Numerous plants hung from the roof gutter, making its original function an impossibility. A rusty stain down the corner served as a reminder of its futility.

The boy parked his bicycle against the gatepost. It was a gatepost which bore no gate, and there was barely enough room to pass. He could not know that Reilly had abandoned the treacherous late-night struggle through his thorn-infested pathway many years ago. He now crawled through a gap in his back fence and awkwardly scaled his neighbour's galvanised gate whenever he came or went.

The boy, book of tickets in one hand and blue biro in the other, struggled through the swamp of greenery in front of him, until he arrived at a mahogany front door, its base black with damp. A saucer once used for cat's milk sat under the fractured windowsill, an immobile spider presiding over its centre.

He knocked on the door, his fingers feeling the hardness of the wood, which sent a small signal of pain to his brain. There was no answer. However, the boy knew Reilly was at home – he was never anywhere else except the pub and that didn't open until half seven. It was only just after four. He stood, looking around the site, wondering what it would have been like in its heyday, when Reilly was a young man and his mother was still alive. The boy's father had told him that Reilly was once an excellent tradesman. One of the finest in the county. He had built the house himself, only employing some labourers. He had made a great living as a local builder in the fifties and sixties. But like many, Reilly had succumbed to the 'aul' drink'. 'Too fond of it,' the boy's father had said. Reilly had progressed from a few relaxing pints of stout on a Friday evening to becoming an ever-present fixture at McGovern's Public House. He had become messy.

A common scene was Reilly in a confrontation over an alleged unpaid bill. He was often to be found in the centre of the front lounge, holding his own kangaroo court. His voice raised towards a bemused local; stubbled, half-smoked Major in one hand, tightly held pint glass in another, a mouldy shirt hanging outside loose trousers. The dripping beer creating a small pool near Reilly's untied boot on the wooden floor. By the seventies, Reilly, then in middle-age, had lost most of his clients, mainly due to rows in the pub. The locals murmured that Reilly couldn't hold his drink anymore. He began raving, talking in riddles. People who had known him in his prime shook their heads slowly and moved away when they saw him coming. Others just laughed, and used Reilly as a light-hearted conversation topic of a Saturday night.

Reilly became less interested in his appearance. Grime and unmentionable stains became a regular feature of his attire, and he gravitated towards the small snug at the far end of the pub where he drank alone. There, in wonder as a child, Reilly had watched his father and friends thirstily slurp stout and half-ones. It was where Reilly had made the torn leather-topped stool with metal armrests in the corner his own. It was where he had sat every night of the past twenty years, since long before the boy was born.

Yet to his credit, Reilly had bought a ticket last year, and the boy had sold two of this current book, so he knew a sale was likely here, if he could find him. The previous meeting had been amicable. The boy recalled a lighthearted grin of Reilly's, while a ball of saliva drooped from the old pensioner's lower lip. He pictured the large woollen sock Reilly had conjured from beneath the tattered sofa in his kitchen and the pile of coppers he had spilled out onto the table. He was, indeed, more forthcoming with his purchase than some of his neighbours, only once inquiring if there were 'fair good prizes'. A good deal easier to deal with than Mrs. Rainsworth, who wanted to give the boy six free-range eggs in lieu of the 50p, or Joe Craddock, who told him that the club committee, of which the boy's father was the chairman, were 'a bunch of aul' gangsters'.

There was a noise somewhere within. A scraping, banging noise. The boy peered through the dusty front window. He rubbed the glass but could see only a dirty lace. He tried again to make a satisfactorily loud knock on the old door, but the result was merely an insignificant thud. He moved to the glass and rapped it as loud as he could.

The light breeze died away. It seemed the world had gone to sleep. The boy looked around as a hush seemed to roll across the winter landscape. The crows perched silently on the telegraph lines, defining the horizon. Maybe Reilly was getting dressed, he wondered. Perhaps that was the noise he had heard. Reilly falling out of bed. It was said that he fell into the drain that ran along the boreen most nights on his way home. The boy imagined Reilly struggling to put on his old musty clothes and looking out the window to see who the unexpected caller was.

It was strange how the world looked different when a person had to wait. A circular pool of water in a field of bog rushes lay like an enormous pound coin, one of those which had only come into circulation in the last year. The line of telegraph poles along the boreen overlooked Reilly's cottage. Their small galvanised rungs attached for maintenance men, two each side and one below, created a sly, smiling expression.

He walked along the cracked footpath. At the side was a windowless gable. Behind the cottage was a mish-mash of bread crusts, old potato skins and tea-bags. The boy thought about abandoning Reilly. It had been a good day. Still, another sale here could bring his earnings to five pounds. He looked in the back window. The kitchen table, where twelve months before Reilly had offered the boy a mug of tea from a questionable-looking teapot and a 'few bishkits,' occupied the middle. A worn flowery tablecloth covered it. Above, a box of tea bags was half open. A brown wrapper clung half on and half off a sliced brown loaf. A yellow Harp Lager emblazoned ashtray spilled with crushed cigarette butts. A tall fridge was in a corner, a worn sticker on one side proclaiming 'Montreal 1976'. The boy could hear it hum.

But there was no sign of Reilly. He looked at the sofa behind the table for a clue. Two cushions lay at one end, some foam spilling out of one. Beside them, the familiar woollen sock that Reilly had used last year. Coppers were around it, he could see more within. Reilly had been getting the change ready, he guessed. He knocked on the window.

'Hello? Walter?' he said. His voice seemed strange against the backdrop of the silent landscape. The boy walked towards the back door which faced him as part of a small built-on scullery. He pushed it and it opened slowly. It stopped less than half way and the boy quickly found that it was jammed by numerous bags of rubbish. He walked inside. The kitchen seemed more neglected in the sharper definition on the other side of the glass. Something crackled under his feet. His eyes quickly followed a trail to a broken whiskey bottle near the peeling wall. He looked again at the sock. Perhaps Reilly was unwell and wanted him to collect the 50p. Reilly had been friendly and more accommodating than most. Indeed, now he thought about it, Reilly had given the boy 20p for himself. He doubted the old man would accuse him of theft, not if he left the ticket on the table.

He walked over and, looking around once more, picked up the coppers, counting them as he did so. To his surprise he reached 50p without the need for them all. He slotted them into his jacket pocket and, sitting on the hard chair, wrote out Reilly's name in the blue biro. He tore off the ticket, which bore details of the New Year's Eve draw and dance in the Community Centre, and placed it on the table, even though it was highly unlikely Reilly would attend.

'Just leaving your ticket here, Walter,' the boy said. He got up and walked towards the back door again, eager to leave the dead quiet of the house. As he reached the scullery, he looked into the hall. The bedroom door was half open. The boy felt compelled to walk down the hall. Something was wrong.

He looked towards the front door. A smell of old clothes wafted through the air. 'Left your ticket on the table, Walter,' the boy said. He found himself hoping for an answer. 'For the raffle.' He walked on the creaking floorboards, passing the converted toilet, the former bedroom of Reilly's sister, emigrated to foreign lands many years earlier.

He reached the bedroom and looked in. On the floor Reilly lay, unmoving. His eyes were open but they were still. The boy dropped his biro. It made a loud 'clack' when it hit the linoleum floor. A small stream of blood had trailed along Reilly's jaw and was drying quickly.

'He's dead,' the boy said aloud. For what seemed a long time he could not move. He eventually turned to the front door and noticed his fingers shaking as he twisted the latch. The cold air offered relief as it hit his lungs.

The boy decided to submit Reilly's ticket to the draw in spite of his passing. His mother said if the old builder won the top prize of £250 it could be donated to a mental health charity or an Alzheimer's disease support group. His father mused it would be fitting if Reilly won the spot prize of a bottle of Jameson. The committee might have a drink in his memory, he added jovially.

But Reilly's ticket didn't win anything. On the night, the boy, sipping a coke, stared at the hundreds of stubs in the base of the drum. He wondered then if some tickets, like Reilly's, were always destined to remain unpicked.

DRENCHED

TRISHA MCKINNEY

My sister Holly's belongings are on her bed. Four neat piles of clothing and the navy holdall she bought in the army surplus shop back in June. I watch her packing the way I would a boxing match. One part transfixed, the other pulling away. And I think to myself, next time it'll be me.

'I'm not staying with them,' I say.

Holly lifts her jumper and places it in the bottom of her bag. Her jeans and tracksuit go in next. I turn my face towards the wall. There is a swell pushing against my ribs.

'You'll be fine.'

I've pulled the sleeve of my top so much it has a hole now running down the inside seam. And I think, 'Nothing will ever be the same.'

We share a room: two single beds separated by a battered white dressing table. The sort of place that's easy to leave. In the alcove there's a hawthorn stick with a cluster of metal hangers and two polka dot dresses we wore when we were kids: blue and white for Holly, red and white for me.

All summer, Holly's planned departure had been closing in, silent and thick as sea mist. The more she tried to train me, the worse it got. With every failure came flashes of insight into some weakness or other in my own character.

I wasn't able to handle him and her, Jack and Jill, Mum and Dad. Holly could. That summer I discovered I was more like them: cowardly and unable to make decisions.

They were Siamese-bound by alcohol: their minds and bodies shrivelled from booze and cigarettes. They looked out onto the world through brittle faces and the world looked back in disdain. Their skin was so dehydrated I wanted to soak it in something clean and pure. 'Yeah. Petrol,' Holly once joked after they'd been on a five-day binge.

Over the years I'd stood by and watched her pour whiskey down the sink then fill the empty bottle with tea. In winter, she would close the curtains at four o'clock in the afternoon and tell them it was night. We walked around in our pyjamas, to try and make it real.

She did things and faced the consequences.

She was brilliant.

But it changed one night while I was doing my homework at the kitchen table. They staggered in around nine o'clock. Within minutes, she was snoring in the armchair, her broken mouth open. She was his wife first, our mother second, though Holly said she could remember a time when it was the other way round.

He was on the sofa opening and closing his legs. I'd seen him at it before: getting himself all worked up for nothing. He started telling me I was the best-looking girl in the whole of Leitrim.

I had one eye on the door, just in case he started playing with himself. Holly said he was harmless and she might have been right, but I didn't want to be stuck in the room with him. The wind slammed the rain against the window pane so hard I flinched. I felt sort of beaten. I could hear his legs moving in and out in a frenzied rush, see his knees coming together and separating. The words on the page blurred in front of me from too much staring – the sides of an equilateral triangle are equal to ...

He called her name. 'Ella, Ella. Are you sleeping?'

She didn't answer.

I could see his zip bent upwards in a semi-circle. The cloth of his trousers stretched taut with the pressure.

Then he looked at me like I was somebody else.

A crevice opened in my chest.

'What's going on here?' Holly opened the door and threw her voice across the room like a disc: flat, round, lethal. His legs locked and his head dropped.

'What are you saying? Is that you, Holly?'

'Oh for God's sake fix yourself up.'

I started to laugh.

'Come on,' she said, and, turning to him, 'we need money for chips.'

'Hey?'

'We need some money,' she told him. 'For dinner.'

'I haven't a penny left.' He tried to jam his hand into his pocket but it didn't fit. He took it out again and let it hang limp.

'There might be something in here.' Holly prized the handbag free from our mother's clutch.

'That's your mother's.'

'I know,' Holly answered, taking a fiver out of a packet of tissues.

'Get your coat,' she said, 'you're skin and bone.'

We walked the mile and a half to the town and ate our chips on the bridge wall. The wet stone seeped through my jeans, but I didn't care. It felt like I'd just won something.

'I'm not going to be around for much longer. You need to be able to handle them. Do you hear?'

'What do you mean?'

'College, hopefully. If I get the points.'

'I'm coming with you,' I said.

'You can't. You're too young.'

'I'm not staying on my own with them.'

'All you've got to do is take charge,' she said, punching my arm.

Everything felt different after that. She made me practise being more like her. I tried to take control but they just laughed or got mad at me for being cheeky.

'You have to be firm with them.'

'I can't do it,' I told her, after another botched attempt at playing the parent. 'I'll find my own way.'

Her exam results came out in August. She didn't get the points. I was sad for her but relieved too. I thought she would have to repeat the last year of school, but Holly had other plans.

'I'm getting out of here,' she said. 'Plan B is Australia.'

'Where will you get the money?'

'I'll go to London first. Get a job.'

'But how will you ...'

'I have a stash,' she said. 'I took a few coins here and there. Over the years it built up.'

'Are you serious? How much?'

She laughed. '892 euro. You should start doing the same.'

Two weeks later I had a new bank account and €12 to get me started. Holly said it was time for her to go. I walked her to the end of the road. We almost hugged when the bus came to a stop, but we changed our minds.

'You take care of yourself,' she said. 'I'll write as soon as I find a place to live. I'll be back for Christmas.'

I watched the bus pull away and felt my insides had been scooped out. I lost my appetite.

I stayed in my bedroom for two days looking at the new lock she'd insisted on putting on.

'Make sure you use it. You don't know what sort of characters they invite back half the time.'

I started sleeping in her bed and looking over at mine, pretending I was Holly and it was me that had gone. By the time her first letter arrived I had written half a copy book in return.

Halloween came and went. I was counting the days to Christmas, trying to ignore them as much as I could, but they didn't like me 'down in the room'. What are you doing down there?'

'Studying.'

'You can study here in the kitchen where we can keep an eye on you. You can't sit locked up there all the time.'

I did as I was told.

Then a Christmas card saying she wouldn't be coming.

'The flights are too expensive. I'll earn more if I work over the holidays,' she wrote. 'I should have enough for my ticket to Melbourne in the New Year.'

It was too much. I couldn't face Christmas. I wasn't strong. I started thinking about the video we'd seen in school. It was about a Christmas tree that went on fire. The sitting room was burnt to nothing in 47 seconds. In less than a minute it was all over. The temperature rose to 2,000 degrees Fahrenheit.

'Heavy smoke builds up and makes hot gas,' the presenter explained. 'The sofa is normally a good source of fuel.'

I was thinking how much easier life would be that night I walked into the sitting room.

His arm swung out in my direction. 'Come over here to me.'

I watched him glance over at her and laugh.

'Don't mind your mother. She can't take her drink.'

I took a step closer. 'Can I have a cigarette?'

'Don't tell me you've started already.'

'Just sometimes,' I lied.

'Take a few,' he said, holding out the packet. Maybe he saw it as a sign of friendship – having a cigarette with your fourteen-year-old daughter. I held my hair back and moved towards the flame of his lighter. He lit one himself.

I coughed.

'You're not able for the strong ones yet,' he laughed. He seemed pleased about that. Something to be superior about.

I took a drag and blew out as much smoke as I could.

I watched his eyes close and his head bounce up and down as he fought sleep, then his chin came to rest on his chest. His cigarette burned between his fingers.

I just stood there for a minute, my mind made up. Then I dropped my cigarette into the ashtray and slid it under the sofa. I took the coat Holly had left for me and shut the door tight. Then I walked a mile and a half to the town in search of a warm bag of vinegar-soaked chips and sat on the bridge until every last one was gone.

WORSHIP   RUTH QUINLAN

Your white shoes aren't white at all. They're just cream pretending to be white and when you hold them against the Communion dress, they look old and discoloured even though you know they're new.

'They're lovely, pet. Why the sour puss?' your mother asks. But you look at the floor and slouch off to your bedroom to sulk. Your best friend's shoes are prettier and they're *really* white.

Later, your mother tries to cheer you up by offering to knit a little cardigan for the dress and you say OK. By then you feel bad for sulking, especially since she spent all Saturday afternoon at the shops, trying to find shoes for your stupidly long feet.

She starts knitting the following week after buying the wool from Mrs Byrne in the knitting shop. Her needles click together, steadily creating something beautiful from the downy, snowy balls. You're only allowed to touch the cardigan once and when you run your hands over it, it leaves mere whispers of sensation on the school-bag calluses of your hands. You have to glide it across your cheek to really feel it. After long periods in your mother's lap, the yarn smells like her perfume.

The small Communion prayer book, with its front picture of Our Lady, has become one of your most treasured possessions. You keep it in the lace drawstring handbag that came with the dress, just to make sure that the mother-of-pearl cover doesn't chip before the big day.

Ever since your First Confession, you've done your best not to dirty up your soul. You've tried hard not to want things you can't have and said extra prayers every night to thank Jesus that Mam saved enough housekeeping money for a new Communion dress. But you're pretty certain that you've been coveting your friend's shoes. And being in love with your own Communion dress probably counts as worshipping false gods. Or maybe it's adultery. But you heard that kissing had to be involved somewhere for that one and you definitely haven't done that to your dress.

The dress, with its stiffened underskirt and the veil-on-a-comb, hangs in your parents' wardrobe. The wardrobe has a small, in-built heater to keep out the damp, which means that the clothes inside are always slightly warm. The whole outfit is sheathed in clear plastic, and whenever the longing to see it becomes too much, you sneak into their room to crack open the wardrobe, just a little. It hangs there, like a promise.

***

Normally, you only have a bath on Saturday night but on this occasion your mother switches on the immersion on a Tuesday, the evening before the church ceremony. She mutters to herself about the cost of hot water. You started having baths by yourself last year but you let her come into the bathroom to wash your hair. You're still not great at rinsing the shampoo properly and you don't want to get suds in your eyes.

The following morning, you sit up on the high stool in the kitchen so that your mother can fix your hair. You want flicks like Charlie's Angels. But your mother starts getting frustrated trying to curl your poker-straight hair; she only managed to convince the hairdresser next door to lend her the tongs for half an hour.

'Jesus, will you sit still. You're like a jack-in-the-box.' She pushes your head over to one side with her finger so she can get a better angle.

'But it's burning me!'

She jerks the tongs away from your earlobe.

Your father comes into the kitchen, smelling of shaving foam. He smiles at you and comes up to kiss your mother on the cheek and as you watch, the deep furrow between her brows smoothes out just a little. He grabs some old newspapers from the pile stacked on the counter. Like every Sunday before mass, you know that he will lay them flat in the back garden and sit cross-legged to polish his brown leather shoes until they gleam.

'Liam, will you bring the dress and shoes up to her bedroom when you're finished?' your mother asks, looking up briefly from her task.

'Sure, love. Are they still in our room?'

'They are, yes. The shoes are at the bottom of the wardrobe. They're still in the box.'

'Back in a few minutes so,' he says, disappearing outside into the sunshine.

When your mother has finally finished styling your hair to her satisfaction, you jump down from the stool and run to the hallway mirror.

'I love it, Mam!' you shout back to her, gently smoothing the curls and preening in front of your reflection.

'Come on, we need to get you into that dress fairly sharpish. Your dad is driving us down and doesn't want to be stuck looking for parking at the church.'

In your bedroom, she carefully removes the dress from the plastic and unzips it down the back. She gathers the skirts and hunkers down to hold them out in a wide circle in front of you. Leaning on her shoulder, you step into the dress and she zips you up. You wriggle around to try and get comfortable in the stiff material before shrugging on the knitted cardigan. Your mother then gathers some of your hair together at the crown of your head and pins the comb into place, adjusting the attached veil so that it spreads across your shoulders. You struggle to bend over the skirts of the dress so she kneels to help pull your lace-topped socks up tight to the knee.

Just then, your father knocks on the door and enters the room. With two fingers of one hand hooked into the straps of your shoes, he dangles them out in front of you.

'I just gave them a quick wipe to shine them up. Do you want me to put them on for you?' he asks.

You nod and he goes down on one knee, easing a shoe onto each foot before buckling them both carefully. Catching a glimpse of yourself in the mirror, you hardly recognise the girl staring back at you. Both of your parents are kneeling; you are the only one standing. Things feel upside down and you're not used to your mother and father looking up at you like this. You remember a picture of the Virgin Mary from your prayer book, her clothes Daz-white and shining as she blesses the children genuflecting to her. You wonder if her parents ever knelt before her like this and whether she felt as you do now.

THE HOLIDAY PHOTOGRAPH   PADHRAIC HARRIS

Ted pours himself another whiskey and fingers the photograph. It is badly creased, with the edges bent a little. He looks at the happy faces. An instant captured ten years earlier. December 19th, 1998.

They are in a restaurant, eating pizza, Playa del Ingles. The four of them on their first sun holiday together. They had been dropped off at their apartment and checked in. They were tired but decided to have something to eat before going to bed.

The photograph records the first and only night of that holiday. There he is leaning in close to Sandra, the two of them smiling, their eyes distracted by the twins pretending they are dropping pizza into their mouths as they recline head to head across the table. They wanted to get up first thing next day to buy buckets and shovels and head for the beach. Ted said, 'Then it's off to bed early, you scallywags,' and he asked for the bill. Sandra was pale and looking forward to getting a tan. Ted told her she could get an all-over one here and she laughed. 'I just might do that if you do too.'

The photograph says nothing about all of that. It says nothing about what happened afterwards or beforehand. Ted has played it out in his head almost daily since that night. They were confused as they exited and unsure if they had come from the left or the right. They were tired. 'I think that's us across there,' he remembers saying, pointing to the Sol apartments. 'Are you sure?' asks Sandra.

Ted recalls how he said, 'I'd better get some water,' and stopped at a street stall. 'We'll head across,' said Sandra. Ted handed the stallholder a banknote but he asked him for something smaller. Ted reached into his pocket and held out his open palm and told the vendor to count out what he needed. The man was picking through the coins when it happened.

Ted used to recount it a bit differently in the early days but he is certain now that this is how it happened. The last time he saw them Sandra was holding a hand of each of the girls heading for the edge of the wide footpath. The girls were hopping and Sandra's head was at an angle as if she had just looked back. There was a screech of brakes. That is all he remembers with any certainty. He recalls a lot of screaming but he can't be certain if it was the girls or onlookers. The only certainty was that the girls, his lovely Sandra, Jenny and Patricia, were dead; there was no doubt about that at any stage. There were streams of blood, scattered shoes and Sandra's handbag. The police and ambulances seemed to arrive immediately. There was a stench of rubber. They had looked the wrong way and walked out in front of a taxi.

Ted had to stay on for a few days to make the arrangements and to speak to the police which, as Ted says, is routine in such cases. The questions were stupid and pointless. The girls had walked across the road in front of a taxi. That was that. Nobody was to blame. It happened. It could not be undone. Of course if things had been different, if they had looked the right way, if somebody had hailed the taxi further up the road, then it might not have happened. The police asked if there had been a dispute with the stallholder about small change. They asked him if he had shouted at the man and if Sandra had called back urging him to come on. No, certainly not, no, that did not happen, he told them. They wondered if that was why, according to some witnesses, her head was turned as she crossed the road. They said she was almost there. They mentioned a bus but he was certain it was a taxi. They asked him repeatedly where exactly he was at the moment when the girls were hit. He told them that Sandra and the girls had gone ahead of him and he was running to catch up with them.

What did it matter now? Ten years on he should be getting over it, he knew he should. Nobody was to blame, it just happened. If he did not get into a shouting match with that man at the stall? Yes, he admits to himself, they did have words but there was no shouting, not enough to distract Sandra, they were not that loud. He told the man to hurry up but the man misunderstood him and was a bit annoyed.

Thomas, his brother, is on the phone. He is giving out to him. 'But you promised that this year it would be different, that it wouldn't be like other years, that you would come over here for the evening, that you would let the story go.' 'I'm trying,' says Ted, 'but it won't go away.'

It's good of Thomas to remember the anniversary, he never forgets. Ted will ring him later before he goes to bed, like he did this morning, and tell him he is fine and is looking forward to the films on TV over Christmas and how he bets Thomas envies him his peace and quiet with the house all to himself and they will laugh and talk for a while about football or small stuff.

Ted prefers to spend the evening alone, in his thoughts, with the photograph, recalling over and over in his head, each time a little differently, the events of that night. He once said to himself it would nearly have been as well if he had rushed after the girls and pushed them out in front of a bus or a taxi that night, at least then the police could have blamed him and locked him up. That might have put an end to it. But no witness gave that account of things and back then there was very little CCTV. He remembers going around the place trying to find cameras so that he could say to the police, 'Check out that camera, it might show what happened.'

It is strange, he thinks, how some people can live with the knowledge of their guilt and it doesn't seem to bother them. They justify things as being for a cause or somebody else's fault, saying, 'They had it coming to them.' Then there are those like me, thinks Ted, who did nothing wrong but blame ourselves even when something is clearly an unfortunate accident.

He remembers the Spanish newspapers. They got it so wrong. They said Sandra stood there waiting at the side of the road, that she looked around at Ted and jumped in front of a bus while holding the girls' hands. That is what they said, the scum that they are. 'Scum, the lot of them,' he shouted to the empty kitchen. Sandra had no reason to do that.

He pours himself another whiskey and, leaning back on the chair, he sees it all. He remembers. They are in the restaurant. He orders a beer. Sandra has a coke. The girls drink orange. They order a big pizza. They are all tired. Fights can happen at times like that. They argue over something silly, it could have been about anything. It could have been about the note she had found in the suitcase when she was looking for her shoes. 'That is there a long time,' he assured her. The waiter, seeing the twins with a camera, asks them if they would like a photograph and they all pose. He remembers now that yes they did have a fight, he had forgotten. A little misunderstanding was all that it was, they quickly patched things up and kissed. Then he asked for the bill.

LOVELY BOY   MADELINE PARSONS

It's the most wonderful surprise to wake in the night and discover my lovely boy still sleeping next to me, his chest rising and falling, rising and falling. I want to kiss his face, his hands, his silky hair, but I don't want to disturb his sleep, so I satisfy myself by inching closer and inhaling his smell – the faint perfume of yesterday's cologne overlaid by the salty tang of new sweat. It's like ambrosia to me. I settle myself on my pillow, lay my hand on his thigh and close my eyes.

I was born in this room, in this bed, even. I remember my mother telling me about it. It was an easy birth, she said, and afterwards the midwife wrapped me in a swaddling blanket, and tucked me in next to her, just like my lovely boy, here. While he sleeps on, the house creaks around me. A few fields away I can hear a dog barking, and in the distance the faint roar of cars on the motorway.

When I wake up he is standing next to the bed with a cup of tea. He has his jacket on. I hold my arms up to him, to embrace him, but he says he has to be going. He's driving to Bury St Edmunds today, to an auction, but he will be back soon. He leans over and kisses my forehead, tells me to go back to sleep, it's early yet. But when I hear the front door close I get up and go to the window, to wave goodbye. He's leaning into the boot of his car, wrapping some things in a blanket, pictures I think. I open the window and call to him. 'Goodbye ...' his name trembles on the edge of my universe, but I cannot call it down.

He looks up at me and waves. 'Goodbye, Moira,' he says, 'and thank you so much, sweetheart. I'll see you very soon.'

At twelve, I hear a car pulling into the driveway. It's my daughter, and I am ready for her; bathed, perfumed, and dressed, hair beautifully arranged. A lady does all that sort of thing for me – an Indian person, I think, I don't remember her name. Emma lets herself in, and comes to where I am sitting in the drawing room, looking out into the garden, waiting for her. She hugs me as if she fears I will break and looks anxiously into my face.

'How are you?' she says.

'Fine, darling, marvellous.'

'I'm sorry it's been a while, Mum; work is frantic at the moment, and the children! Please tell me I wasn't as difficult a teenager as my two.'

'You were a model child, darling. Not a bit of trouble, ever.'

She laughs. 'I'll tell the little devils that when I get home.' She takes off her jacket and settles herself next to me on the sofa. 'Has Jamila been coming as arranged?'

'Yes, she has. She's wonderful.'

'I'm glad.'

She turns to me then, her brown eyes searching my face, and holds my hand. Her forehead creases into a frown.

'I've been talking to Dr Bennett about you, Mum,' she says. 'Remember I took you to see him last month?'

'Oh, yes. Yes, of course.'

'He suggests that we look at photographs together to try to stimulate your memory, you know? Shall we do that? Perhaps just for half an hour or so, before we go to lunch?'

'Of course, darling, that would be fun.'

She goes around the room and takes down photographs from the mantelpiece, scoops up a few from the piano and lines them up on the coffee table.

'So,' she says, 'let's start with this beautiful lady.'

I gaze at the woman smiling out from the frame. She is wearing a black dress that comes down to her ankles, and is sitting in a raffia chair in a garden, a shawl around her shoulders, squinting into the sun. On her knee is a child of about two years of age, with fair curly hair and a shy smile. I think I know who the old lady is, but her name won't come.

'Give me a clue, darling.'

'Don't worry, Mum, it's not a competition. And it doesn't matter if you get it wrong; the important thing is to try.' We gaze at the photograph together. 'Any ideas?'

'Well … I'm not sure …'

She squeezes my hand and beams at me as if she is presenting me with a fabulous prize. 'That's you with your granny Fitzpatrick,' she says. 'Remember how you used to talk about her all the time … that lovely house she had in Dublin? Sandycove, wasn't it? Your parents took you to visit her every summer? She used to bake Victoria sponges, and rhubarb crumble, and she made the most wonderful scones? When I was a child you used to tell me about your granny, and her cooking, and how she loved you very much.'

The big kitchen in Sandycove: door open to the summer sun, a cat lounging on a window sill, and at the end of the road, the sea, gleaming. Or is that just a picture I saw in a magazine? I close my eyes and it comes to me: the sweet, tart smell of my grandmother's gooseberry crumble in the oven; the gust of Cusson's talc rising off her papery skin as she kissed me goodbye before my parents took me back to England. I think I remember. I think so.

Emma takes up another photograph. A dark-haired man stares back at me, handsome nose, smiling mouth. Middle aged. He is standing proudly next to a young woman with long, fair hair dressed in an academic gown. He has his arm around her. I stare at them for a long time.

'That's you, Emma,' I say, 'of course.'

'That's excellent, Mum,' she beams, 'and who's that standing next to me?'

I look at him for a long time. I feel I should know him, but his name won't come. But it's not my lovely boy. That I do know.

'I'm not sure, darling,' I say.

'Oh, Mum.' Her diamond rings flash as she raises her hand to brush away the tears that have suddenly spilled onto her cheeks. 'It's dad; your husband, Andrew. Do you not remember him at all?'

'Of course I remember him, darling, of course I do. Really, these glasses are absolutely hopeless.' I take her hand. 'I do remember him.'

I try to conjure him up. Dark head next to mine in my soft feather bed, smiling mouth, strong white teeth. Andrew.

Emma holds another silver-framed photograph towards me. 'This is you and dad on your wedding day.'

I take the picture in my hand. There's that man again, a younger version of course. He looks as if he should still be in school. My husband. And beside him a girl, dressed in a white dress, her arm linked through his. My daughter says it's me, and I don't doubt her word, but as I stare at my young face smiling out at me, I cannot help thinking: who is that person?

'You used to tell me that was the happiest day of your life, Mum.'

'It was, darling. Very happy.'

'I couldn't have wished for a better father,' she says. 'And you and he were so happy together.'

'We were, darling. Very happy.'

She puts the photographs away, says we have done enough for one day, and that we should get going. She's taking me to Mario's, she says, the new Italian restaurant that's just opened in town. While I pop into the downstairs lavatory she runs up to fetch a different jacket for me. She doesn't like the one I am wearing – the navy would be better, she thinks. She is gone for some time. I am standing in the hall waiting for her when she comes down the stairs, her hand to her mouth, her face flushed and blotchy. She is carrying a brightly coloured garment on a hanger.

'Have you been ... seeing someone, Mum?'

'Seeing someone? No.'

'Then who owns this shirt that I found hanging in the wardrobe? There's other stuff up there too. And it's not Dad's. We gave all his clothes to the Samaritans after he died, remember?'

'It's ... well, it's just my lovely boy who comes to see me sometimes, darling ...'

'Your lovely boy? Who's he?'

I want to tell her, but his name won't come.

'And he sleeps with you, doesn't he?'

The way he gathers me to him, and strokes my breasts, and kisses my neck, my mouth, my eyes; the precious weight of his body on mine, loving me. I want to tell her, but the words won't come.

'Oh, Mum,' she says, 'how long has this been going on?'

A long time, I think, but I cannot be sure. I say nothing.

She takes her mobile phone out of her bag and presses numbers on it. She tells me to go into the sitting room and to wait for her. I hear her in the hallway: *but you must tell me if my mother has overnight visitors, Jamila ...* I don't listen to any of the rest. When she has finished speaking, she goes upstairs again. She is gone for a long time. I wait for her in the sitting room and stare out into the garden, at the beds of roses bursting into bloom. It is the most glorious summer day.

***

We have left the windows open so the night air can cool our naked bodies. My lovely boy lies on his side next to me, his hand resting on my stomach, and starts to drift into sleep. I take his hand, and kiss it, then turn on my side, pulling his arm around me. He gathers me to him and pulls me closer. We make spoons. I feel his breath on the back of my neck like a blessing. To be able to reach out and touch him as he lies sleeping next to me is all I ever want for the rest of my life.

We do not hear the car pulling up to the house, or the front door being opened, or the group of people coming up the stairs and opening my bedroom door. When the light is suddenly switched on, and we sit up in fright, there is Emma glowering from the doorway and some other men I don't recognise. One of them yanks my lovely boy out of the bed, throws him some clothes and tells him to get dressed. He stands by the window, clutching them, looking ashen, the brown of his forearms a vivid contrast against his pale chest.

'Wait a minute,' he says, 'please … let me explain; it's not what it looks like.'

'Yes, it bloody well is,' Emma says.

I sit in the bed, holding the sheet to my chest. I want to say something, but the words swirl above my head, and I can't call them down.

'I'm sorry, Moira,' he says to me.

'Shut up!' Emma barks at him. 'I have an inventory of everything you took, you prick. I'll prosecute if they are not recovered within thirty days.'

He turns to me. 'But they were gifts, weren't they, Moira? They were gifts. Tell her.'

I hear them bustle him down the stairs and into a car, the crunch of pebbles on the drive as they take my lovely boy away. I hug his pillow; it smells of him, of the lemony cologne he always uses. I get out of bed and stand at the window, stare at the road that leads to the motorway, listen to the hum of traffic in the distance. I stand there until I see the sun begin to glint on the windows of the houses on the hill opposite and the birds burst into a clamour of singing. The scent of roses rises from the garden. It's going to be a beautiful day.

POETRY

CRUSHIE

BREDA WALL RYAN

The rain has stopped. Sunlight
veneers a table set between windows.
The year turns.
To the south: a window half-filled
with pewter lake topped with pine and naked sky.
The window to the west leans out to frame
a pair of toxic yews, the native kind.
A foal-at-heel runs to brood mares grazing the field.
Its pliant hooves drum light as raindrops.

Behind the house, men clear herbaceous borders,
burn snapdragons and red hot pokers,
the acrid tang of bonfire clings to scarred thornproofs.
A gravelled path munches boots.
In jeans and scarlet gansey, a woman
rakes leaves into drifts she shovels
onto a rust-scabbed wheelbarrow.
The rake's tines are worn to stubs,
its beech handle slips through her palms,
polished by generations of hands.
She barrows leaves over a weathered oak plank
to the fire on the kitchen-garden terrace.

At the bottom of a steep slope
a wooden boathouse stands at the water's edge,
glazed black and reeking of creosote.

A pontoon of oil drums floats on the cold flat lake.
Here all is motionless: air, pontoon, water,
the far shore's fringe of yellowed spruce,
its reflection.

Below the surface, invisible pike hang suspended.
It is like winter: still, cold, relentless.
It is like death.

Near the house, at the top of the slope,
the season turns. The wind burns,
woods blaze to burnt sugar and molten jazz.
Beech and birch broadcast pale coins
across the shivery grass.
They dull to tarnished brass
the way a grushie flung from chapel steps
is diminished
by the splendour of the bride.

Grushie is a traditional wedding custom in Ireland and Scotland where the best man throws handfuls of coins to spectating children after the ceremony.

THAT HOUSE GILES NEWINGTON

I wake at four. I'm seven again.
Did that house ever truly exist?
Chug of the rumoured nuclear train,
cellar stairs ending in an extra twist?

Did that house ever truly exist?
Coal fire, oval mirror, candlestand fingers,
cellar stairs ending in an extra twist,
purr of the era's sultry singers.

Coal fire, oval mirror, candlestand fingers.
My dad's Don Draper, my mum's Liz Taylor,
purr of the era's sultry singers,
babble of triumphant artistic failure.

My dad's Don Draper, my mum's Liz Taylor,
lashed to the mast in their London square,
babble of triumphant artistic failure,
fits of the vapours in the smoke-stained air.

Lashed to the mast in their London square,
fits of the vapours in the smoke-stained air,
sirens crooning, Armageddon looming.
I wake at four. I'm seven again.

COCKLE PICKING — AMANDA BELL

Look first for an open cockle shell,
spreadeagled on the damp part of the strand,
then, with your fingers, form a claw,
to dredge through the soupy layers of the sand:
below the meniscus, bunched like fists,
their little clumps feel weighty in the palm.

It rained when I brought you cockling –
how fast the mist erased you from my sight –
then you happened on the picture-postcard
seaweed man, who stopped his ass-cart,
asked you for a light.
You leaned in, not expecting
him to seize you, or the strength
with which he held you, like a vice.

I think of you whenever I go cockling,
soft and shivering in your crackling plastic mack:
you thought he'd hide you under piles of gleaming seakelp
while he waited for the cold tide to flow back.

LOVE WITHOUT MEMORY — MAURICE DEVITT

Some days her words will fill
a thimble of sense and you will think
the gears are catching, thoughts
no longer slipping like paws on ice.

That maybe you had called
the grassy separation too early.
Names, once too fragile to touch,
she will pin to faces. Talk will spin

the wheels of reminiscence, her mind
racing through the history of a life,
not yet over. As you leave
and she clasps your hand in her spidery grip

don't be surprised
if she whispers her sister's name.

THE NIGHT OF SAINT LUCY'S DAY   D.S. MARTIN

with inspiration from Dante, Donne and George Mackay Brown

Black   the night descends   scarcely seven hours
from when it crept away

Who was this luminous saint   whose legend sings
of faithfulness in the darkest day?

Seven bright leaves in the winter tree
whose roots are frozen   brittle branches thin

Light glitters on the sea   a silver star
an eye plucked out that caused no sin

Night walks with heavy steps
echoes deep loss   the things that are no longer

A child leads her candlelit procession   stronger
than darkness   enabling all to see

Clouds of warm breath   crystallize in the cold
She is the enemy of all cruelty

FUAMNACH MAKES A MOTH OF ETAIN   ANN EGAN

All is quiet here now.
I've given that lot their orders.
They're to pile high the fire
with seasoned logs gathered

as the moon dipped beneath the hill.
Day and night they're to tend it.
I must away to my foster father.
I can't bear to listen to Etain's cries

of pain as she leaves this world
for a space beyond our living.
Would I could be done with her
but Midir surely would find out.

I had to settle for her changing
into a nondescript insect,
a moth of the air to lie maybe
on the underside of a branch,

fly aimlessly in the gloaming,
crash into sparks of fire.
A thing of no repute nor renown,
some misbegotten grey fly

unable to battle winter woes,
face the frost of purple evening.
I have enough of her.
I had my work cut out

manoeuvring her to my bride chair.
You'd think there were forces
holding her back even as she crossed
my threshold on my husband's arm.

His arm, that's my place to be.
She is silly enough to believe
I'd welcome her to my palace.
My stronghold, silver sparks at sunrise,

scarlet gleams at moon's setting.

LOUISE LATOUR

PATRICK MADDOCK

I type in your name: the search engine finds
a small aphid which originated in California
and spread through the vineyards of France
like wildfire from 1860 onwards…
I know this isn't you, Louise, and feel
no need to visit any other forum,
checking who lays claim to that name.
To me, you are always fourteen:
you have hobbies, play tennis,
and like listening to music. You suffer
from toothache and *mal à la tête*,
the *rheum* and the *grippe*. In your country
one *hirondelle* doesn't make a Spring.
It doesn't say what religion you are –
Catholic, breathing a scent of the Little
Flower? – you, my earliest exotic.
You are not language lab and look a bit
peaky, in keeping with the stilted script.
Maybe it's loss of blood – my sympathies –
but in Albert Folens' French, you are love's
young face waiting to be expressed.
He carries you here on a wan air,
grants you a comic-strip sort of existence.
For a sweet while, we're *in camera* –
the book has me *tu*-ing you in my head:
you sip from a glass, legs uncrossed
on my three-foot-wide bed, passing
through loops certain letters make.
But we are under-age: you, dark-eyed
and fringed; me, in my broken tongue.
For an avid spell, you slip out and in,

almost a summer girl I meet at Irish college;
you have a pen-pal I don't wish to hear about.
But I sense you are not long for this, Louise –
how soon our world will abandon you,
allow you to vanish off course, since it
makes business sense and the future's
a new shady place, bearing captions
and photos, until a girl runs clear out of ink.

TULCA — AIDEEN HENRY

Irish for wave, gust, gush, outpouring, flood, deluge.

Sacrum and sternum in gold,
both keystones, crowns of arches,
reciprocal.

They embrace pressure from each side,
disseminate impetus, uncoil movement,
crossways

up through the body from the kicking foot
or down from the throwing arm
symmetrically

through the body when the butterfly kick
pitches head and winged arms
up out of water like a rising angel.

AN GHAOTH ADUAIDH — FIONA NIC DHONNACHA

Tháinig tú ar nós an ghaoth aduaidh
Agus an ghrian
Ach ní mealladh milis a rinne tú
Ach séidigh le straidhn
Ag stroiceadh, strachailt, ciapadh
M'anam, m'intinn á tharraingt ó chéile
Mo lochtanna nochtadh, náirí
Ag gaoth chomh géar le fuip
Fágadh gan mothú
Mo chroí stollta
Ag do ghaotha garg, ghoimhiúila
Méaracha fuairnimh ag scríobadh cnaipí m'anam
Ach níl aon biseach ón ghaoth aduaidh
Istigh mo chnámha, tríd mo chuid féitheacha
Táim oscailte, amh
Ag an ghaoth aduaidh

D'imigh tú ó dheas arís.
Níl fágtha ach an ciúnas.
A fhágann an scrios.
Agus sceall folamh chráite.

GOODBYE AND HELLO — ADAM WHITE

All week long you talk of passports, planes, foreign exchange,
of not leaving the bags until the last minute
(as if all holidays began with the *challenge*
of getting away, and everything that's in it),

of saying goodbye at the office.
Then, in the restaurant, on our last night there,
people, names we're moved to mention, seem the fonder
for being spoken of at such a distance.

Home again, coats hung in the hall, emptying the phone
of messages, you say one, like bread and butter
somehow, wouldn't be the same without the other:
the getting away and then the glad to be home.

NECROMANCER   AMY BLYTHE

An empty vase, a hot water bottle
and tacky mumbo jumbo
were your contribution, leaving
all other bits and pieces to my discretion.
I was in charge of the what-ifs
leaving you to master sleeping
it off. You did say you'd be there.
I did take it for granted that you lied.
It's understandable to get lost
in the hocus pocus
but unforgiveable to be found
wanting for the sake of it.
       Pace
past all the pretty little dead things
lining the floor.
     Follow the red line
to the exit.
   If the sun doesn't rise,
we can find a place with fluorescent
lighting.
   If the night doesn't turn,
we can hope to be the only ones left
alive.

BY THE LANDING'S LIGHT — C.P. STEWART

I open the pitch pine door, look in on you.
In your bed by the window, sleeping tight.
Darkening curls on a white pillow.

Those twelve black panes – no curtains there.
Outside, that steep climb to the moors;
the stars.

Behind you the cow jumps over the moon.
I had forgotten that – so long ago.
On the floor your book, your pen, your knife.

Would you know what is coming?
I could tell you now.
The road you chose, the way we came,

to this last house; this winter's night.
By the landing's light, I watch, you sleep.
Six, maybe seven; and all still well.

TO YOUTH   BRIAN KIRK

The day will come when you will want to leave
your home and family and your friends behind.
You will not stop to wonder or to grieve,
new days will open out inviting blind
pursuit of dreams that probably won't come true,
or if they do, then not the way you planned.
Yes I am old and cynical, but you
are young; a year is just a grain of sand
that falls unnoticed in your hourglass life.
Success is so apparent you can taste
the wine, hear the applause, ignore the knife
that warns of hurt to follow, interlaced
with tears and laughter, boredom and the rest
that makes our lives so blundering, so blessed.

ON READING THE GLOSSARY ON
THE LICHENS OF IRELAND WEBSITE   SINÉAD COTTER

He's anxious to examine my apothecium, my disc.
His specialty is lichens; my specialty is him.

He languidly studies my ascus, my pores,
and fondles his way round my areoles.

No conidia here! My fruiting body
is raring to go, but is it a hobby

for him, is it love or just specimen-hunting?
(My hyphae aren't perfect; my medulla's lumpy.)

Are we haploid or diploid? Unpaired or together?
The lure of my propagule won't last forever.

We're reaching symbiosis. Is it parasitic?
Or can I dare hope for mutualistic?

Is that it? Is he leaving? My squamules are leprose.
My podetium's wilting; my thallus is crustose.

He can shove his green algae where the sun never goes.
More vegetation? A single red rose.

RECOMPENSE

JEAN TUOMEY

To be so full and filled
after nights seeing the black sky
slip into light,
hearing silence shift to birdsong.
Books, radio, emergency numbers
at arm's reach, oblivion arriving at 7am.

To share these bright days now,
purpose rippling out and out,
ease moving in and in,
sleeping through the dawn and its chorus.
Locker cleared and feeling blessed;
blessed to feel blessed.

WINTER GEESE — OLIVIA KENNY MCCARTHY

I mark the sky with winter geese –
this scattered trellis of wings
lifts me from the tumbled dahlias
and smooth stones, where my secateurs
snip out the end of autumn.

I drift with them in a deep sky –
a cool prayer thickening on my tongue –
my fingers coiled round dead stalks
the blown buds of late roses.

Evening incense flares in me
kindness worries like a friend
when long distance my eldest daughter's voice
becomes a river under a wooden bridge,
a cliff terrace with a view of red roofs
a halo of evening lights –

it is the tinkle of a bell
sharp slant of winter sun on water.

IN SLEEP

MARIA BENNETT

You are scattered across my dreams:
at Keem Bay heading for the Atlantic
you kick at dried seaweed

and sail from me in a red boat.
On a beach after midnight,
there's a fire in the distance,

hooded boys don't frighten me
as much as your silence.
I wake and dress without thinking of clothes.

You put a black rose in my hair once,
I had a slim taste of you, more salty
than any man I knew.

Keep pouring water
and we won't be able to wade.
Swim. I wear dresses made for selkies,

have no doubts, and know you can sail alone.
Keep me till later, you said,
keep me till the tide goes out,

until they all go home.
When you kissed me I caught a cold,
but I know you always bless me when I sneeze.

RINGSEND WATER MUSIC, 1983 — EAMON MAC UIDHIR

At river high tide on the hot days
Grey mullet graze the undersurface.

Nearby, at the old canal lock,
Corduroy boys strip to divebomb,
Smashing the pane of the afternoon.

Above it all, an effortless gull
Pursues a sinister aimless purpose,
And over there, harassing the sun,
Swifts sift the air for midges.

I whistle for the ferryman
– coming about at The Gut –
And leap for his glancing gunwale.

Charon would have waited, you know,
If it was my time that had come.

TREACLE

FIONA SMITH

Tunnelling through treacle, trying to place –
To remember – a flat in Dublin,
In Baggot Street (or was it Portobello?)
On a June evening when we were young.

A room with a cracked ceiling in the flat
Of a friend, someone you knew in Harold's Cross
Or somewhere around that part of the city.
It was a balmy night and I saw the stars

From the open window of that dim room.
How could that have been possible?
With all the city lights reflected in the sky
Above that space, with its cistern crooning.

Nothing else sang. There were no nightingales.
No square below. But we had the stars.
We didn't dwell on them, being young
Was enough for us on a June night.

You went out for fags. We all smoked then,
Finding a place that was open until 2 am,
Long before all-night petrol stations,
Back in half an hour to that crooked couch.

There was a fruit bowl on the kitchen table
With nothing in it. Apart from one rotting core.
There must have been a drip, the failing drone
Of a fly trapped somewhere in that flat.

It may have been near the Bleeding Horse,
Or The Barge. The crash of beer bottles,
Shouts, jeers, the crack of a broken nose,
Engines running into the jitters of dawn.

SEASALT AND WOODSMOKE   RACHEL BROWNLOW

My lungs are made of an ocean
That swirls through my throat.
Its waves have been leaving seaglass
Remains for years,
I think that's why my words
Are sometimes broken.
I think that's why my eyes change
From green to grey
In the light.

You were born in the earth.
Your feet firmly planted,
Soil spilling from your ears.
If you peeled back your hair
You would see a map of veins,
Leaf skeletons etched across your skull.
Your voice crinkles like autumn
And when the air is cold enough
To make your breath hover in clouds,
Then you taste like ice and
Cinnamon and woodsmoke.

You have never seen the sea,
Even though it surrounds me.
If you were submerged you would drown
But I need it to breathe,
If you lay me in the earth
I would dry out,
The colour leeching from my skin.

But we are steady,
Your roots encircling our feet.
You can keep me together
And I will crash my waves.
I will be the rain
That keeps us growing,
Because without each other
Water and earth would crumble.
Without each other
We would both sink.

CARTOGRAPHY — LUKE MORGAN

They begin the intricate act of pin-
pointing the surface of your skin into
a 2-D, immovable country on the monitor
where the psychedelic colours
of the body's temperatures and breathing motions
could be a weather forecast or an elevation study.

Tracing the region borders between nape
and collar-bone, shoulder and ulna,
they find what they're looking for North,
a few kilometres-to-scale
below of the jawline straight as a continent-
edge;

a raised hub of land, hard as moss-covered flint,
and with tools that can be likened
to rulers, brass compasses, pencils
sharpened to scalpel-tips,
they mark it with an 'X',
begin planning the dig

while I struggle at reading their chart,
no wiser than I ever was
at understanding the map
of your road systems, tiny estuaries –
not knowing which way is up or down,
East, West.

BONE — TIMOTHY MCLAFFERTY

Desiccated relic of our appetite,
the wishbone gathers dust on the sill

above our sink. My wish would be to have
never pulled it from the roasted flesh,

or that we didn't relish eating birds
grown and sold in boxes; but we hunger.

And what fitting penance for such desires?
And why this one guilt among the many?

Why not run clean as the wolves with their
destruction left far behind them? And so

I differentiate the mind of man
from that of animals, but not the needs.

RHAPSODY IN BLACK — MARK HART

I

Jet-black, opaque smoke from a stubble-burn
smudges the air and drifts across the highway.
Cars and trucks pass in and out
through a veil between worlds.

Under blue sky, soot-flakes are falling.
The charred lake of the field smoulders,
two dimensions without depth
swallowing light. A rim of fire

grabs toward dry tinder
as it eats itself homeless, brief-lived.
Where the plough has turned over fresh soil,
flashes of orange lap against a limiting shore.

II

A murmuration of starlings comes –
peculiar, Pointillist cloud

independent of wind, gyrating, then
a sudden budding forth of cinder leaves,

the incoherent, of sound of
empty glass jars dumped into a barrel,

a shimmer among furrows,
bobbing, scratching, gleaning fallen seed.

III

The living room at night
mirrors in the picture window,
familiar shapes and colours

but darker,
dimmed and dulled by the
unseen other side.

SCRIBBLES

MICHAEL FARRY

Shall I compare our scribbles on placemats,
paper napkins, parking tickets and
receipts from bank machine withdrawals?

My words are desperate, jagged
speculations on diners engrossed
in themselves, delicate dishes cooling

or on imagined lovers isolated
in the front seats of public transport,
miserable, dreading the next stop.

My scrawls bear no fruit. At night
when I type them up their banality
demands deletion, their tawdry plots

the commonplace of cheap fiction,
soaps and films where the music
suggests more than the lame dialogue.

Yours, I imagine, in a neat, tidy script,
disjointed maybe, but making sense
in the uniform slope of letters and assurance

of the handwriting. I see your notes
blossom later, sentences fill out with
juicy detail, punctuation click into place,

the characters reveal their names,
back stories, while you uncover
their darknesses and the plot

thickens into unexpected wisdoms.
I await your finished poem,
your full story, the unscrawling of scripts.

TULIPS

JANET SHEPPERSON

'The tulips should be behind bars, like dangerous animals' – Sylvia Plath

Dismantle the cage. Now they're too old to bite.
The petals should be brown, smelling of ditch water;
they should have sagged and fallen weeks ago.
Instead they perch defiant, like winter birds
each at the top of a tall, straight tree, clenched up
against an unseen wind that tosses and carves them
into outrageous shapes. Flames frozen in air.
Gargoyles. Driftwood. Chinese paper lanterns.
The ribs of a boat rising slowly out of the sand.

Once they were curved like eyelids, smooth and glossy,
soaking up sunshine, perfect little consumers,
purring. Now their colour is leached away,
they are only texture, brittle and ridged as sea shells.

No more red roaring. Just a russet sigh,
too weak to eat up anyone's oxygen.
But still they cling without scent or juice or hope
like barnacles abandoned on a rock,
tideless and dry and holding on for ever.

The petals are prised apart, the light shines through;
they are curled and shrivelled under its strident weight.

Bloated with memories of gold and scarlet,
engulfed by withered leaves and crackling stems,
I see my own face peering through the bars.

NECROMANCER

CHRISTOPHER MEEHAN

Holding court north of Moher, a path beaten through
Rock and bramble,

A henge of upright Solids, the picture will show
A giant boulder,

There is warmth through a cup in cold hands –
A slow passing shower,

You, me and the farmer's dog watched night –
That lunar Necromancer,

Pull the moon up from the brow of the islands as
The sun fell away from

The curvature of the earth.

KILL YOUR DARLINGS   BETSY BURKE

Sadness pours over the barely there barrier
from the mouth of the train – her whistle is

childhood, her tracks rusted shame, and I
am a suicidal copper penny of after school

games – kick-the-can and no man's land
and let's play mommy and daddy, while I

am, *so am*, I am green eggs and ham, with my
mother's hands on my shoulders, her words

in my mouth, *You never let anyone touch you there, you hear?*
And I did. It happened to her, and maybe the sounds

of a train were distant that day – her whistle childhood,
her tracks rusted shame, and I am of a sadness that will

never be written away.

THE CANALS ON MARS — EAMONN LYNSKEY

A part of scientific fact so long,
the canals on Mars. Authenticated by
our leading men, our leading journals, books
describing in fine detail waters funnelled
from the polar caps in summer, feeding
verdant plains and setting out sharp
crannied images discerned across
a forty million miles of lifeless void:
hard evidence a race of engineers
had harnessed nature to its purposes.

What boats went bobbing on those surfaces?
What barges ploughed the channelled waters of
that red Atlantis? What the navigators
steered what skiffs between those cliffs cut out
from solid rock? Could we have met those peoples,
bringing only peace this time? Not come
as conquerors but cousins, not invaders
out to steal their lands, not harbingers
of death and devastation but intent
on sharing ingenuities and skills?

We might have made a sort of late amends
for our Pizzaros, Amhersts, all the pain
endured by new-discovered nations. Might have
left behind our histories for once
and landed on their dusty, arid plains
with nothing in our plans but good intentions.
Might have had another chance to prove
we could be human and humane at once
among those alien peoples we believed
had etched canals across the face of Mars.

LOOK UP SHANNON QUINN

Eat dirt
A chaser for the anxiety of swallowed stories
Sink into topsoil
Secrete enough sadness to soften your bones

Somewhere the ocean gives back
A piece of glass
Someone picks it up
Sees splinters of a life never lived

Beast of an idea
How much we think we matter
How very unlovely it becomes

Yellow dog with big brown eyes
Takes his old determined joints
Out for a sniff and a piss
Walks right over you
Look up
Pick a prick of light to pin a prayer on
Brittle stars move sideways
Choose carefully

SQUARE PEGS

MARK O'FLYNN

How many photographs does it take
to make a building fit for human consumption?
A thousand pictures could be a school, a bungalow.
A thousand words a convict brick.

How many happy snaps does it take
to piece together a yellow brick road?
My pixelated face leans to yours
and together we build our little world.

They say there are as many bricks
in existence as photographs
which seems a curious comparison,
like monkeys typing Mozart.

For every round peg a square hole.
I've heard three thousand bricks, roughly,
to build your average domicile,
but who's doing all this counting?

Is a brick digital? Is the image physical?
Your pixelated face leans to mine
and together we breathe as one lung.
Are there as many knives as forks?

Or as many shower heads as car keys?
How many arias compare to mousetraps?
Probably enough is the equation.
How long then will love last?

It's all so much tilting at wind farms
making these strange declarations,
developing an *is* from a *wants-to-be*,
as many in-breaths as exhalations.

POSTCARD FROM TASMANIA — MARK MULLEE

A bird they call the currawong disturbs
what little sleep I get. It's not at all
like home. Even when I find a place that serves
a drink you'd know, it's poured in what they call
pots and schooners. The clatter of the train
is loudest after dark; around the corner
it shunts from track to track. A week of trying
to learn the muddled names of streets has worn
me out. The more I learn, the less I mourn
the recent past. They say a race now half-
extinct once farmed this land with fire, to lure
their prey with young and supple shoots, a whiff
of burning scrub to them like baking bread
to us. The fire gone, grass grows there instead.

Biographical Details

Amanda Bell is a freelance editor and doctoral student in UCD, where she currently tutors on Coming of Age Narratives. Her poetry has been published in *The Stinging Fly*, *The Burning Bush 6* and the *Ofi Press Literary Magazine*, and was shortlisted for the Mslexia Women's Poetry Competition, 2013. She is a member of the Hibernia Poetry Group.

Maria Bennett recently graduated with an MA in Creative Writing. She has been published in *The New Writer*, *Envoi*, *Orbis*, *Crannóg*, *Boyne Berries*, *Prole*, and *Pickled Body* and has poems forthcoming in *Poetry Bus*, *Ink Sweat and Tears* and *Antiphon*.

Amy Blythe lives in Kildare and works in a stationery firm in Citywest. Last year, she completed a master's degree in Creative Writing at Queen's University Belfast. She has previously been published in *Crannóg*.

Rachel Brownlow is a nineteen-year-old student from Cork. She is in her second year of studying Creative Writing in NUI Galway. She writes poetry and fiction.

Betsy Burke studies literature at the University of North Carolina at Greensboro where she is earning her BA in English. Her poetry can be found online and in several literary magazines including *The Bastille*, *The Coraddi*, *Dead Snakes*, *Willows Wept Review*, and *The Write Room*.

Sinéad Cotter won the Hennessy First Fiction Award (writing as Sinéad McMahon) in 2003. Her poems have been published in the *Sunday Tribune* and *Irish Independent* and on the *Poetry 24* website. She is currently working on her first collection of poetry.

Joe Davies' fiction has appeared in magazines in Canada, the UK and the US, most recently in *The New Quarterly*, *The Missouri Review*, *Queen's Quarterly* and *Planet – The Welsh Internationalist*. He lives in Peterborough, Ontario, Canada.

Maurice Devitt completed the Poetry Studies MA at Mater Dei in Dublin. He was recently shortlisted for The Cork Literary Review Manuscript Competition, the Over the Edge New Writer Award, Westport Arts Poetry, The Doire Press International Chapbook Competition, and the Listowel Writers' Week Poetry Collection Competition. He was nominated for a Pushcart Prize in 2012. He has had poems accepted by various journals in Ireland, England, Scotland, the US, Australia and Mexico. He is a founder member of the Hibernian Writers' Group.

Ann Egan has held residencies in counties, hospitals, schools, secure residencies and prisons. Her books are *Landing the Sea* (Bradshaw Books), *The Wren Women* (The Black Mountain Press), *Brigit of Kildare* (Kildare Library and Arts Services) and *Telling Time* (Bradshaw Books).

Michael Farry was selected for Poetry Ireland Introductions, 2011. His first poetry collection, *Asking for Directions*, was published by Doghouse Books in 2012. He won the Siarscéal Poetry Competition (Roscommon) and the Fermoy Poetry Competition in 2013. He is also a historian and Four Courts Press published his book, *Sligo: The Irish Revolution 1912–1923*, in 2012.

Padhraic Harris has participated in creative writing classes at GMIT. He was a featured reader at Over the Edge in Galway in September 2013. He lives in Galway where he practises law.

Mark Hart's first collection, *Boy Singing to Cattle*, won the 2011 Pearl Poetry Prize and his poetry has appeared in *Atlanta Review*, *RATTLE*, *Poetry East*, *Margie*, *Tar River Poetry* and *The Spoon River Poetry Review*. A native of the Palouse region of eastern Washington State, he now lives in western Massachusetts where he is a psychotherapist, a Buddhist teacher, and a religious advisor at Amherst College.

Antoine Josse was born in 1970 in the west of France. He grew up in Brittany, in Vannes, right beside the city of Lorient, which is twinned with Galway. He now lives and works in Normandy and carries his suitcases full of images and sounds to expose his paintings and sculptures locally and on to Paris, Switzerland, Chile and the US.

Martin Keaveney has been published in *Gold Dust* magazine, *The Galway Review* and in the Poddle Publications anthology, *Small Lives*. His screenplays have been screened at national festivals, including the feature-length *Paper Rich* at Galway Colours festival, 2012. He is developing a pilot based on mythical Irish legends for Room 12 Productions in London. He works part-time as an academic writing tutor at NUI, Galway

Seán Kenny's fiction has appeared in *Crannóg, The Irish Times*, New Irish Writing in *the Irish Independent, The South Circular, Southword* and *Wordlegs*. He won the 2012 Over The Edge New Writer of the Year competition, was placed third in the 2013 Francis MacManus Short Story Competition and was shortlisted for a 2013 Hennessy Literary Award.

Olivia Kenny McCarthy has had poems published in *Cyphers, The SHOp, Crannóg, Peregrine* (USA) and *The Stony Thursday Book*.

Brian Kirk has been shortlisted for many awards including Hennessy New Irish Writer Awards in 2008 and 2011. His stories and poems have appeared in many literary journals and anthologies. He was selected for the Poetry Ireland Introductions Series in 2013. He blogs at: http://briankirkwriter.com/

Eamonn Lynskey has published two poetry collections, *Dispatches & Recollections* (Lapwing, Belfast, 1998) and *And Suddenly the Sun Again* (Seven Towers, Dublin, 2010). He recently obtained an M.Phil. in Creative Writing from Trinity College Dublin.

Mary Rose McCarthy's stories have won or been placed in numerous competitions such as Swanwick Writers Summer School (UK) competition (1st) (2007), The Amergin Awards (2nd) (2007). She was long-listed for the Penguin Ireland/RTE Guide short story competition (2010) and (2013) and came first in the Kenny/Naughton short story award in 2010 and The Lonely Voice in 2011. She won the Golden Pen short story award in 2013. Her work has been published in *Woman's Way, Ireland's Own, Cork Evening Echo* and in *Cork Library Arts Service anthologies* (2008) and (2009).

Trisha McKinney has read her work at the Lonely Voice Short Story Competition and was shortlisted for the Michael McLaverty Short Story Competition in 2008. She won the RTE Guide/Penguin Ireland short story competition in 2013 and was shortlisted for the Bord Gáis short story of the year award.

Tim McLafferty lives in NYC and works as a drummer. He has played on Broadway in *Urinetown, Grey Gardens*, and many other places. His poetry appears in *Barrow Street, decomP, Painted Bride Quarterly, Pearl, Portland Review* and elsewhere. His website is www.timmclafferty.com.

Éamon Mag Uidhir is a Dubliner living in County Kildare. He has had poems published in print in *Revival, Crannóg, the moth, Caterpillar, THE SHOp* and *Cyphers*, and online at *Burning Bush II* and *Misty Mountain Review*.

D.S. Martin's poetry has been published in Canada, the USA, Australia and the UK in such publications as *Anglican Theological Review, Canadian Literature, Christian Century, Dalhousie Review, Sojourners* and *Spiritus*. His poetry books include a chapbook, *So The Moon Would Not Be Swallowed* (Rubicon Press) and two full-length collections, *Poiema* (Wipf & Stock) and, *Conspiracy of Light: Poems Inspired by the Legacy of C.S. Lewis*. He is the Series Editor for the new Poiema Poetry Series from Cascade Books.

Patrick Maddock is a former Hennessy Poetry Winner and was shortlisted for the Inaugural Gregory O'Donoghue International Poetry Competition. His poems have appeared in various magazines in Ireland and England. A sample of his photography appeared in this year's Eigse Festival in Carlow.

Christopher Meehan was shortlisted for the Fish International Poetry Prize in 2012. In 2013 he was placed third in the Over The Edge New Writer of the Year Competition. His poems have been published in *Skylight 47*, *Boyne Berries* and online in *The Galway Review*.

Luke Morgan has had poems in *Poetry Review*, *Poetry Ireland Review*, *Cyphers*, *Crannóg* and *the moth* amongst others. He is currently being considered for the Hennessy Award.

Mark Mullee was born in Houston, Texas, and currently teaches English in León, in the north of Spain. His poems have previously appeared in *Crannóg*, as well as *Poetry Ireland Review*, *the moth*, *Borderlands*, and *Improbable Worlds*, an anthology of Texas and Louisiana writers.

Siobhán Murtagh is a native of Dublin, now living in Co. Kildare. Her stories have received Honourable Mentions in New Millennium Writings 2012 and The Seán Ó'Faoláin International Short Story Competition 2013. She has been shortlisted in the Carousel Writers Competition 2013. She is currently studying Creative Writing for Publication at NUI Maynooth.

Giles Newington was born in London. In 1996 he moved to Dublin, where he works as a journalist at *The Irish Times*. He has been shortlisted in a number of poetry competitions and was published most recently in *Abridged* magazine.

Fiona Nic Dhonnacha has just completed an MA in Literature and Publishing. She writes poetry and short stories in both English and Irish.

Mark O'Flynn is an Australian writer. He has published four collections of poetry and three novels. His first collection of short stories was published in 2013.

Madeline Parsons' stories have won prizes in competitions and have been published online and in anthologies. She is currently working on a collection of short stories. Born in Dublin, she lives in Westcliff-on-Sea, Essex.

Shannon Quinn lives in Toronto, Canada. Her poetry has appeared in *The Literary Review of Canada*, *Ruminate*, *Thin Air*, *Sand*, *Halfway Down the Stairs* and *Southword Journal*.

Ruth Quinlan was shortlisted for the 2012 Cúirt New Writing fiction prize, longlisted for the 2012 Over the Edge New Writer of the Year competition, and won the Hennessy First Fiction Award in April 2013. She was also a Featured Reader at the February 2013 Over the Edge: Open Reading. Her work has been published by the *Irish Independent*, *Emerge Literary Journal*, *Thresholds*, *SIN*, *Skylight47* and *Scissors and Spackle*. She has also contributed to three anthologies, *Watching my Hands at Work: A Festschrift for Adrian Frazier* (fiction), *Abandoned Darlings* (fiction) and *Wayword Tuesdays* (poetry).

Janet Shepperson has published poetry widely, most recently in *Poetry Ireland Review*, *Cyphers* and *The Stinging Fly*. She has also published short stories, two of which have been shortlisted for Hennessy Awards. She has published pamphlets with Lapwing Press and two full collections of poetry, *The Aphrodite Stone* (Salmon Poetry, 1995) and *Eve Complains To God* (Lagan Press, 2004).

Fiona Smith is a translator and journalist. She has had poetry published in *Southword* and in the Hennessy New Irish Writing page of the *Irish Independent*. She won the 2012 Over The Edge poetry competition and is currently shortlisted for the Cork Literary Review manuscript competition.

Rebecca Stiffe is a seventeen-year-old writer from Galway. She is currently studying Journalism and New Media in the University of Limerick.

Jean Tuomey, a former teacher, facilitates creative writing groups in Mayo. She trained as a writing facilitator with the National Association of Poetry Therapy in the United States. She has been published in *The Stony Thursday*, *Crannóg 33*, *Fish Anthology*, 2011.

Breda Wall Ryan was awarded joint third place in the Patrick Kavanagh Awards and won the iYeats Poetry Contest, Poets Meet Painters Competition, Dromineer Literary Festival Poetry Contest and Over the Edge New Writer of the Year, 2013. She is a Pushcart nominee and lives in Bray.

Adam White worked as a carpenter/joiner in Ireland and France for many years before reading English and French literature at NUI Galway. He has recited his poetry at venues in Galway, Tipperary and Cork, at the Electric Picnic, and at venues in England, Italy and France. His first collection, *Accurate Measurements*, was published in April 2013 by Doire Press in Connemara and shortlisted for the Forward prize for best first collection.

Stay in touch with Crannóg

@

www.crannogmagazine.com

Lightning Source UK Ltd.
Milton Keynes UK
UKOW04f2201130214

226442UK00002B/39/P